James H. Waggoner

© 2018 by James H. Waggoner. All rights reserved
No part of this book may be reproduced, stored in a retrieval system, or transmitted by any means without the written permission of the author.
Published by Author James H. Waggoner 2/24/2018
Print book is printed on acid-free paper.
This is a work of fiction. Names, characters, businesses, places, events and incidents are either the products of the author's imagination or used in a fictitious manner. Any resemblance to actual persons, living or dead, or actual events is purely coincidental.

ISBN-13: 978-1986435789
ISBN-10: 1986435784

Dedication

To Debra and Lillie. You two are the epitome of love. Debra, our love has always been on the sibling level instead of cousins. Lillie thanks for making that call in May of 1998. You changed my life forever.

To my Children, each day you do something amazing that makes me proud to say I'm your dad. Keep up the great work.

To God, from whom all blessings flow, without your unselfish love and guidance none of this would be possible. To my family and friends, you are the greatest and I appreciate all of your support. Each of you has your own unique way of challenging me and keeping me grounded.

James H. Waggoner

Chapter 1

Thank God it was the last day of this senseless conference. All week long the presenters spoke on outdated equipment and software. Our beloved Government was always a few steps behind when it came to technology. I sat through most of the meetings multi-tasking and thinking about Maxwell. We had never been apart for this long and I missed him.

I had two projects to complete when I got back to Washington D.C. I tried to work on them while I was here, but the remote access connection wasn't the best and let's just be honest the Wi-Fi inside of hotels isn't secure. In my world, security was important. My thoughts were interrupted when my supervisor came by.

"Samantha, I hope you've enjoyed the conference." She said.

I lied.

"It has been informative Ms. Cooper."

"Good! I'm looking forward to sharing your trip report with the team." She said.

"I wasn't aware I had to do one." I said.

"Of course you do. The team needs as much information on the upcoming updates as possible." She said.

"Yes ma'am. I will submit it to you for your review before it goes to final."

"Samantha, I trust your work without scrutiny."

"Thank you Ms. Cooper. You've been a great mentor to me and I value your opinion." I said.

She blushed before walking away.

The current session was ending, and I had five more to go before I could head to the airport to catch my return flight home and see Maxwell. I walked over to one of the tables set up with coffee, tea, small bottles of water and pastries. I needed some caffeine in the worst way. I was adding milk to my coffee when I heard a pleasant greeting.

"Good morning."

"Good morning." I said.

"Enjoying the conference?" He asked.

If one more person asked me that question I was going to scream. I smiled and lied again.

"Yes! But I am glad today is the last day." I said.

"I agree with you there. My name is Bryson Garrison." He extended his hand.

"Hi, I'm Samantha Hunt. Nice to meet you." I shook his hand.

"Ouch! He said. Were you trying to squeeze the life out of me?"

"No! I don't like dainty handshakes."

He was still overplaying the hurt feeling in his hand.

"Nice to meet you Sam! Where are you from?" He asked.

"My name is Samantha! I was born in Houston, Texas."

"Are you drinking decaf or regular coffee?" He smiled.

"Regular." I said as I left for the next session. "It was nice meeting you Mr. Bryson."

"Likewise, Samantha."

When I sat down in the next session I saw Bryson walk in and sit towards the front. My supervisor walked in shortly thereafter and greeted Bryson. They both exchanged smiles as they shook hands. I wondered if Ms. Cooper's handshake was dainty. From the looks of it most likely no because I didn't see Bryson display the antics he did at the beverage table with me. The lights dimmed a bit and the coordinator took to the podium and introduced the next guest speaker – Bryson Garrison. He was the Deputy Director of Cyber Security for the Department of Homeland Security based in Frankfurt Germany. He held a Ph.D. from Cornell University and served in the Army for 8 years.

As the attendees applauded after the introduction, Bryson stood and walked to the podium. He was wearing a dark grey two -button suit with a crisp white shirt and blue patterned tie. His shoes were cognac with a fresh shine and he wore an American Flag pin on the lapel of his coat.

When he spoke his voice immediately grabbed the room's attention. His briefing style wasn't like the others of the week. He used very few PowerPoint slides and walked around the room. When he saw me, he continued as if we hadn't just exchanged pleasantries a few moments ago. I liked that he didn't draw attention to me. A professional.

At the end of the session it was time for lunch. The conference included lunch in a different hall. As I walked towards where lunch was being served I was on the lookout for my supervisor to avoid having lunch with her. I needed to check my emails and respond to important ones and this was my only chance to check in with Maxwell. I missed him. I didn't see Ms. Cooper in the hallway. Maybe she went out for lunch today. I filled my plate with two southwest chicken wraps, some celery and two spoonful's of ranch dressing. I grabbed a bottle of sparkling water before heading to an empty table.

When I sat down, I could see the room filling up with other attendees from the conference. I checked my email and didn't see any that needed my immediate attention. Most of the emails were news about the update going live in two weeks. I finished up my sparkling water before heading into the last session. The time flew by and I was thankful of that because I didn't want to drink another cup of coffee this late in the day.

The conference was finally over and lots of people were congregating in the lobby saying goodbyes and passing out business cards. I have been to so many of these that I declined to participate in the farewell gathering and left as quickly as I could. I didn't see Bryson again after his session. The cab ride to the airport was met with rush hour traffic.

I looked at my watch to check the time. I didn't want to miss my flight. I made it to the airport with under an hour to spare before my departure. After I checked my bag I rushed to security and my heart sank when I saw the long line moving at a snail's pace. My face felt flushed and I was starting to perspire under my neck. Just then I felt someone tap me on my right shoulder.

"Ma'am what time is your flight?" The female TSA agent asked.
"5:05 PM." I said.
"Please come with me."
"Thank you."

She led me to the TSA Pre-check line and proceeded to the front. I overheard her tell the male TSA agent checking identification my departure time and to let me ahead of the next person in line. I stood there happy and awkward at the same time. I knew the people behind me were calling me all kinds of names. When he finished checking the person's identification in front of me, he checked mine.

"Not to worry we'll get you to the gate in plenty of time."
"Thank you."
"No problem. Have a safe flight Ms. Hunt."
"You have a great evening."

I turned and apologized to the woman standing in line behind me. She smiled.

"It's okay dear, things happen. Have a safe flight."

I returned the smile.

"Thank you."

I made it to my gate with some time to spare and so I was able to dash into to the ladies room and then grab a hot tea from Starbucks.

Chapter 2

I was so frazzled trying to get through security that I didn't even write down the names of the two agents who helped me. I wanted to send a letter to their supervisor. You normally get major attitude from TSA agents instead of the customer service I received. I made a note to contact the airport to see if they can narrow down who was working that security area at that hour. My flight home was quick and turbulent free. As soon as I powered my cell phone on I had voicemails from my mom and my best friend Carrie. I returned my mom's call first.

"Hi Mom! How are you?"

"Hi Sam! How was the conference and your flight?"

My mom is one of the few people I didn't mind calling me Sam.

"Everything was great mom."

"I saw Maxwell yesterday."

"How was he? I can't wait to see him."

"He's fine, being his same old self."

"You know I've never been away from him this long."

"Yes, I know Sam. Are you coming by this weekend? Your father was asking."

"Yes, mother dear I will be by on Sunday. I'll call dad once I get in my car."

"Okay Sam. I'll talk to you soon. I love you."

"I love you too mama."

I started playing in my mom's make-up when I was 2 years old and it never stopped. I'm a girlie girl but I'll shoot some hoops with the guys and have a beer on Monday nights for football! After I hung up with my mom, I dialed Carrie's number as I exited the long term parking lot at Reagan National Airport.

She answered on the second ring.

"Hi Sam! Welcome home."

"Hey Carrie!" Thanks.

"How was it?"

"Same old boring outdated stuff." I laughed.

"Were any handsome men walking around?"

I thought about Bryson. I wasn't sure if I considered him handsome.

"Not really. I knew most of them from previous conferences and they're starting to sit behind the desk too much."

"Oh no! Mid-section crisis." She laughed.

Girl, yes and they still ate donuts every morning."

"Did you leave the hotel and check out the city of Orlando? I heard the nightlife is great."

"No! I should have. I just went to the bar a couple of nights and had some wine. A few gentlemen tried to hold a conversation but the circumference of their bellies was too distracting."

We both laughed.

"Okay Carrie I need to call my dad before I get home. Let's catch up soon. Drinks? Dinner? Or whatever."

"Sounds good girl. I'll talk to you soon."

I merged onto the George Washington Parkway en route to my home in Northwest D.C. The traffic wasn't heavy at this time of night so I cruised easily down the parkway and admired the Nation's Capital in my view. I loved living in the city and all that came with it. I received an incoming call. It was Trent. We met a few months ago and had been out on a handful of dates. It wasn't anything spectacular, but he was kind and appeared to be respectful. We've held hands and kissed each other goodnight after our dates but that was it.

"Hi Trent!"
"Hi Samantha! Are you back from your business trip?" He asked.
"I just landed actually a little while ago and I'm heading home."
"Are you tired? Would you like to meet for tea?" He asked.
I looked at the clock on my dash 8:17 PM.
"Sure, where did you have in mind?"
"How about Baked & Wired"? He asked.
"Sure. I will head there now."
"Thank you. See you soon." He said.

I enjoyed Trent's company, but I didn't feel we had relationship potential. He was great to talk to and an attractive man. On paper he was great but something just wasn't clicking with us. He was an architectural engineer from Memphis, Tennessee. He moved to the District three years ago, had been in a relationship with his college girlfriend until he moved here. He didn't have any children and was an only child but didn't display the typical tendencies. We met at a wine tasting this past spring. He was there with another guy, which I initially thought was odd but quickly ruled out the assumption that he was gay after he asked for my number.

I found a parking space not too far from Baked and Wired. When I reached the entrance, I saw Trent sitting at a small table looking at his phone then I felt my phone vibrate.

"Hi handsome! I received your text when I walked in."
"Hello Samantha! You look great as usual."
We embraced before I sat down.
"So tell me about your conference." He inquired.

"It was okay. I didn't really learn too much to be honest."

"I believe that. You're great at what you do."

He was so complimenting.

"Thank you. You just landed a huge design contract." I said.

He smiled. I could see his dimples.

"Samantha, do you mind if I ask you something?"

"No, what is it?"

"Do you think I'm attractive?"

"Yes. Why do you ask?"

"We've been talking for a few months with little to no progress."

"Trent, I wasn't aware you wanted to date."

"So you assumed I didn't?"

"I was raised not to pursue men and you hadn't asked me to be in an exclusive relationship or even hinted at it to be honest, so I thought you were fine with how things were."

"Are you dating anyone else?"

Now I'm starting to get a little annoyed.

"No I'm not Trent."

He tried to hide his satisfaction, but I could tell he was happy to hear my answer. Where is the waiter or waitress? I'm ready for some hot tea and something sweet now.

"Hi welcome to Baked and Wired. What can I get started for you?"

"May I have a chai tea and blueberry muffin?" I said.

"And for you sir?" she asked Trent.

"I'll have an espresso please." He said.

The waitress repeated our orders and dashed off to the kitchen. I could tell Trent was thinking about our conversation before we ordered. I broke his train of thought.

"So how's the new project coming?" I asked."

His slow response confirmed my thoughts.

"It's coming along. I submitted the 15% design for review." He said.

"That's great. How do you feel about it?" I asked.

"Samantha, I apologize. It's just that."

"Trent no need to apologize. It's called communication."

"I like you but I haven't been in a relationship since my ex."

"No need to explain Trent. It's okay. We're fine as friends. I enjoy your company."

"That's just it Samantha. I want to be more than your friend."

"I'm not ready for a relationship Trent."

"How are you so sure?" He asked.

Truth is I was ready to be in a relationship but not with him. I didn't want to be mean though.

"Trent, can we please enjoy this evening? I haven't seen you in sometime and I don't want our first night to be like this." I asked.

He looked at me intently. I hadn't really noticed his eyes before. They were hazel and complimented his dimples.

"That's fine Samantha." He said.

The waitress returned with our order and we had small talk at best about the cherry blossoms, the Wizards and the current administration. The late night crowd was starting to come in. We finished up and I offered to pay but Trent politely took the bill from me and paid for what was probably our last meeting. When we got outside the cool breeze felt good.

"Where did you park?" He asked. "I'll walk you to your car."

"I'm just up ahead. It's fine." I said.

I didn't want to prolong this any longer.

"Are you sure?" He asked.

I smiled before I replied.

"Yes it's fine, Trent. I had a nice time."

I turned and walked towards my car.

"Will I see you again Samantha?" He asked.

He looked so charming standing there with a slight smile and one dimple showing. I smiled back just before opening my car door.

"You have my number." I said.

Chapter 3

I headed home to see Max where I should have gone in the first place. Perhaps seeing Trent this time was the closure I needed in what wasn't going anywhere. The quiet storm DJ was blaring through my car speakers, and I felt relaxed as I approached Massachusetts Avenue. I turned into my condo-parking garage, and the attendant greeted me.

"Welcome home Ms. Hunt," Patrick said.

"Thank you."

As I pulled into my parking space, my cell phone starting ringing, but the caller wasn't showing yet on the screen. I hope it wasn't Trent. After the next ring, I saw 'Dad' appear on the screen.

"Hi, Dad!"

"Hi, baby girl." That's what he called me still to this day.

"Dad I just pulled into the garage. I'll call you when I get upstairs."

"Okay. I love you," he said.

He told me that every time we spoke.

"I love you too dad."

I got my bag out of the trunk and headed to the elevators. When I made it to the elevator, my cell phone started ringing again. I pulled it out of my purse. It was Trent this time. I didn't want to talk to him anymore tonight. The conversation was uncomfortable in the restaurant, and I was ready to relax for the rest of the evening. After my cell phone stopped ringing, I heard the sound indicating a voicemail was left. I would check it later or in the morning. I was ready to see Max, and I needed to call my dad back.

When I unlocked my door, I could hear the water streaming from my electric waterfall. I spoke out a hello as I walked in and laid my keys on the kitchen counter and sat my luggage down. A week's worth of mail was waiting for me on the countertop. I grabbed a glass from the cabinet to get some water.

"Max," I called out.

Nothing.

"Maxwell, I know you hear me."

Then he came out of my bedroom, slowly walking towards me and stretching at the same time. I knelt down as he got closer and he rubbed his soft white furry body against my leg, and I heard low purrs. I stroked him and told him I missed him as I sat down on the floor. He rubbed his head against my chest. He walked back and forth around my lap. I got Max when he was a year old from a rescue weekend at a local pet store. His green eyes were electrifying, and I knew I wanted him at first sight. That was 4 years ago.

I stood up and grabbed my cell phone before sitting on the couch. I dialed my parents' home number.

"How was your trip baby girl?" my dad asked.

"It was okay dad. I've been to so many of those things."

"And your flight?" he asked.

"Short, no turbulence, thank goodness."

"How's Max? Your mother and I went by and checked on him every day."

"I appreciate that so much dad. He's good, sitting on my lap."

"Any plans this weekend?"

"Carrie and I are hanging out one day, and I'm coming over to see you and mom."

"How's Carrie doing?" he asked.

"She's well."

"Okay, I'll let you enjoy your evening. I'm sure you're exhausted."

"Thanks, dad. I'm going to watch a couple of the shows I recorded."

"Okay Sam. Have you spoken to Trent?"

I told my dad about anyone I was dating because he was the first to teach me about love and how a man should treat me. I didn't want to go into the details right now with him.

"Yes."

My dad knew when I gave one-word answers there was more to the story, but I wasn't ready to discuss it.

"Have a good evening Sam. I'm glad you're home safe. See you this weekend. I love you."

"I love you too dad."

Max was looking up at me as if he knew I had spoken to Trent as well.

"I'm not telling you either Mister," I said as I rubbed him and started an episode of the Blacklist.

When I finished watching James Spader tell his latest target why he was killing him, I listened to Trent's voicemail. He was calling to see if I had made it home safely and didn't mention anything about the conversation earlier. Thank God I was hoping he wasn't calling to explain and go on and on. He's such a nice guy, but I'm going with my gut on this one. I pressed the phone key to delete his voicemail and headed to my bathroom to shower with Max not far behind me.

I lit a mango cilantro scented candle in my bedroom before I showered. Nothing feels better than your own shower no matter how many five star ratings a hotel has. The hot steam immediately made me feel good and relaxed. I should have done this first, but I wanted to spend some time with Max and return my dad's phone call. I washed and conditioned my hair since I had started going natural without a relaxer, I loved my hair smelling good and looking clean. I dried off, washed my face and applied lotion to my body. I left the bathroom the way I came into this world and pulled out one of my dad's old dress shirt from my dresser drawer. I dabbed some Marc Jacobs perfume on each side of my neck and crawled into my bed. I grabbed the television remote and turned to HGTV. Max jumped up on the bed and laid at my feet. A couple in a suburb of Raleigh, North Carolina was looking for a home with a $400,000 budget. Yeah right! I paid more than that for my two bedrooms two bath condo. The three homes they were choosing from would sell in the low one million dollar range in this area. My cell phone beeped twice. I had a work email. Lord I don't want to go to the office tonight. I picked up my cell phone and opened the email.

Hi Samantha. It's Bryson. I wanted to email you to see if you've made it home safely. I didn't get a chance to speak to you again after our brief introduction. I leave for Germany tomorrow afternoon. If you don't mind, I would love to hear your voice again. My number is 714-823-0898. I hope you're home and I hear from you before I depart tomorrow.
Good night,
Bryson.

I was surprised to hear from Bryson, and it felt weird because we didn't exchange information. I was flattered though. The HGTV couple in Raleigh chose the four bedrooms, five bath brick home. I hit the reply button as they were hosting their new home party with friends.

Hi Bryson,
Thank you for emailing me. Yes, I've made it home safely. I hope you have a safe flight back to Germany tomorrow.

Good night,
Sam.

Chapter 4

I woke up and checked my phone to see if Bryson replied to my email. He hadn't. I got out of bed to floss and brush my teeth. Max had moved to his morning spot. My living room window had a view of the city and he fell in love with that spot after his second day with me. I put a pair of jogging pants on, a sports bra and t-shirt and my running shoes. The cool morning breeze felt good as I began my five-mile run around the city. Every weekend I took a different route and the city never disappointed with all walks of life. Today I would head towards Georgetown up towards MacArthur Avenue then back home.

I finished up my run and called Carrie.

"Good morning" I said.

"Good morning Sam." She said. "Did you go running this morning?"

"Of course I did. Five miles."

"I was going to join you but Jonathan came over." She said.

"Say no more. I understand."

"Sam! Girl it keeps getting better." She laughed.

"Really?"

"Honey he read some poetry to me last night. Then gave me a massage."

"Wow! Go Jonathan." I yelled.

"He might be a keeper." She said.

"When you asked me if there were any handsome men at the conference? I sort of lied." I said.

"Details?" Carrie asked.

"Well one of the Directors from an overseas branch was there."

"And?"

"We introduced ourselves and that was it." I said.

"That's it?" Carrie I asked.

"Well…."

"Samantha Hunt!"

"Oh no! Not my full name." I laughed.

"Well what? What happened?" She asked.

"He emailed me last night."

"And said what? Stop playing with me Sam?"

"He wanted to know if I made it home safely and wanted to hear my voice before he leaves today."

"How does he look?" Carrie asked.

"He's handsome." I said.

"Denzel handsome, Matthew McConaughey handsome, Dwayne Johnson handsome?" Come on Sam she said.

I laughed before answering.

"He's a combination of Matthew and Tyson Beckford." I said.

"I'm hanging up so you can make that call."

"Wait a minute. I didn't say I was calling him."

"Why not? Trent? I thought you said that wasn't going anywhere?"

"It isn't but that doesn't mean I need to call Bryson."

I slipped and said his name.

"Bryson?" She repeated. "I like his name."

"Tysons or Chevy Chase?" I asked.

"Chevy Chase. It's supposed to be a beautiful day." Carrie said.

"Okay I'll see you at 1 o'clock."

"Let's meet at Maggianos." She said.

"Sounds good."

We hung up and I stood looking out of Max's favorite window. In the distance I could see planes landing towards Ronald Reagan airport. Down on the street I could see people accumulating taking advantage of the beautiful weather. I felt Max rub against my leg. I knelt down and rubbed him before heading to the bathroom to shower.

As the hot water splashed against my body I couldn't help but think about Bryson's email. It was sweet of him to email me and his message wasn't too aggressive. I didn't get the impression he wanted anything more than a friendly conversation before he left today. I have to admit his voice was sexy and his hazel eyes were attractive. I stepped out of the shower and dried off. Max wasn't present. Just like that things were back to normal.

After I applied lotion to my body I put on a blue thong and bra. Then I picked out a pair of sky blue Capri pants and a white blouse before I sat on the side of my bed. I picked up my cell phone and dialed the number Bryson included in his email. The phone started ringing. He didn't say what time his flight was as the phone rang a few more times. Maybe I've missed him.

"Hello." He said.

"Ili Bryson."

"Good morning Samantha."

"Did I catch you at a bad time?" I asked.

"Not at all. I'm sitting at the gate waiting to board my flight." He said. "Thanks for calling."

"No problem. That was really sweet of you to email me."

"I looked for you after the conference." He said. "Email is so impersonal."

"I didn't want to miss my flight."

"I understand that." He said.

"I don't remember giving you a business card." I said.

"I apologize but I looked you up in the agency directory. Lucky for me you're the only Samantha Hunt." He said.

Proactive!

"Oh okay. How long is the flight to Germany?" I asked.

"7 hours direct to Frankfurt." He said. "Have you ever been to Germany?"

"No I haven't. My high school did a Spring break trip to Switzerland." I said.

"Did you go?"

"Yes it was nice."

"You should put in for a site visit." He said.

"Yeah right. That's all they talk about is budget cuts." I laughed.

"Do you have vacation time?" He asked.

"About three weeks."

"Take a week off and come visit. There are plenty of tour agencies."

He wasn't asking me to come and visit him but to come to Germany.

"How long have you been over there?" I asked.

"A year. Two left." He said.

"Do you like it?" I asked.

"I love it to be honest."

"Love it? Really?" I asked.

"Yes. The culture, the history, the architect and the upkeep of the buildings are incredible." He said.

I could hear the excitement in his voice. A very nice sounding voice at that.

"Sounds like you could be my tour guide." I can't believe I just said that.

"I wouldn't mind but I didn't want to come across arrogant." He said.

Charming with humility!

"Touché!" I said. "And we wouldn't want to upset your girlfriend." I laughed.

"That's funny. He said.

"What's funny? I asked.

"The assumption that I'm in a relationship."

"I didn't mean to offend." I said.

"No problem. I was in a relationship when I first got here."

"What happened?"

"Besides the obvious?" He asked.

"Yes smarty pants."

"Honestly I believe she had unrealistic expectations." He said. "What about you? I hear there's a lot of men in the Nation's Capital."

"Quantity versus Quality! There's a difference. I said.

"Shouldn't be hard for an attractive woman like yourself." He said. I could hear him smiling as he said that. More charm.

"You're a little charmer I see." I said.

"Just stating the truth." He said.

This conversation had gone on longer than I expected.

"How long have you been with the agency?" I changed the subject.

"7 years. What about you?" He asked.

"I started 3 years ago."

"Do you like the agency?"

"Yes I do. I just wish they'd spend the funds to be more innovative." I said.

"Agreed. Have you suggested that to your boss?"

"Come on. You're a director. You should know it's not that easy." I said.

"Our budget is a little different than the stateside operations." He said.

"How so?"

"We're partly funded by the Germans and they're real serious about their cyber security."

"Don't you think America should be as well."? I asked.

"I do. You could be the catalyst to that changed.

Ambitious!

"Well Bryson I honestly didn't think we'd talk this long. I'm meeting a girlfriend and I need to get going."

"You mean boyfriend, don't you?" I heard him laugh.

A little arrogance in him. I like it.

"You're cute. No I'm meeting my best friend." I said.

"Do you mind if I save your number and call you sometimes?" He asked.

The elephant in the room and the FCC were present on the line now. I didn't answer right away.

"Sure, but calling international is expensive isn't it?" I asked.

"Thank you. No it isn't." He said. "Enjoy your day with your girlfriend." He laughed again.

"Have a safe flight Mister."

"Thank you for calling me Samantha." He said. "I agree with you I didn't think this call would go this long."

"Be safe Bryson and send me an email to let me know you made it home safely please." I asked him.

"Can I call?" He asked.

I was chewing on my bottom lip and fidgeting with one of the accent pillows on my bed.

"Email me please." I said.

"Okay Samantha. Have a good one."

"Bye Bryson."

The call disconnected and I exhaled deeply. Talking to him came easier than I expected it would and that scared me.

I got up from my bed and started getting dressed. It didn't hit me until then that I had talked to Bryson the whole time in my bra and panties. I felt weird all of sudden but smiled at the same time.

Chapter 5

I changed Max's litter box and put fresh water and food in his bowls before leaving. When I walked down the hallway I saw Mrs. Clark walking towards me. She was a widow in her 50's with no kids and a successful blogger from Maine.

"Welcome back Samantha!"

"Good afternoon Ms. Clark. Thank you." I said.

"I saw your parents a few times checking on Max while you were gone. They're such sweet people."

"Yes they're great. How are you?" I asked.

"I'm well. Just finished a yoga class at Equinox." She said. "I'm heading up to Potomac for the day."

"Sounds good. I'm on my way to meet my girlfriend Carrie."

"Enjoy. Let's go for tea soon." She said.

We hugged and kissed each other on the cheek. I continued to the elevator to meet Carrie.

When I got to the parking garage my phone beeped twice.

I'm in my seat. It was so nice talking to you Samantha.
Bryson.

I asked him to email when he made it home safely. I shook my head before replying.

It was nice talking to you as well. I asked you to email me when you got back to Germany. LOL.
Samantha.

I know but I just can't believe we talked so long and I could have talked longer. No disrespect but it came so easily. I'll email you when I get home.
Bryson.

Safe travels Bryson.
Sam.

I got lucky and found a parking spot on Wisconsin Avenue not too far from Maggianos. I called Carrie to see if she was here already.

"I see you found a parking spot. I had to park in the garage." She said.

"Where are you?"

"Walking up Wisconsin." She laughed.

"See you shortly." I said.

When I finished parking I saw Carrie standing on the sidewalk next to my car. She had on a pair of khaki shorts with a plum color blouse hanging off her shoulders with a brown wedge heel sandal and a shoulder tote. The sun was barely out but she had on a pair of aviator shades. Carrie was smaller than me and worked out like a fitness model with a Nike endorsement.

I got out of my car and we ran towards each other and embraced in the middle of everyone walking on the sidewalk. We didn't care. "Look at you girl." I said.

"What? Do I look fat?"

"Please you look fantastic." I said.

"Thank you Sam. You look great yourself." She said. "Did you call Bryson?"

"You're funny." I said. "Do I look desperate for a man?"

"Not at all. I was just asking." She laughed.

"Lets go inside and get a mimosa." I said.

The patio seating at Maggianos was perfect for people watching and the weather was just right to keep us looking cute and not sweating. A waiter came and took our drink order.

"It seems longer than a week since we've seen each other." Carrie said.

"I know. Let's not rush today. I missed my girl." I said.

It was eating Carrie up inside to know if I called Bryson or not. She was looking at the menu to distract herself. Although she knew already what she was ordering - a salmon Caesar salad with the dressing on the side, she kept looking at the menu until the waiter returned with our mimosas. The waiter took our orders. Just like I predicted Carrie ordered a salmon Caesar salad with the dressing on the side. I ordered the shrimp Alfredo. That's why she was smaller than me. I loved my pasta. When the waiter left we raised our mimosas and toasted to our ten years of friendship.

"So what are we doing today?" Carrie asked.

"Let's hit our normal stores." I said. "Try on something sexy and enjoy this weather."

"That works for me. I want a new pair of dark jeans anyway." She said.

"To add to how many already?" I laughed.

"They're not as dark anymore." She said. "You know I like my jeans real dark."

"Yes! Just like your men." I said.

"And Jonathan is rich chocolate." She said.

We both laughed.

"Okay girl! Did you call Bryson?" She laughed.

I shook my head and took a sip of my mimosa.

"Yes I called him."

"What did you guys talk about?" Carrie asked.

"He mentioned me coming to visit Germany."

"Wait! I thought you said you guys had a *brief* conversation at the conference?"

"We did." I said.

"So how did you visiting Germany come up?"

"The visiting just came up in general." I said.

"What else did you guys talk about?"

"The agency, changes within the agency. That's it." I said.

"How did the conversation end?" Carrie asked.

"He asked me if he could save my number and call me sometimes."

"What did you say?"

"I told him sure."

Carrie laughed.

"I doubt he'll call me often if at all."

"And that was it?"

I loved her but she was so nosey.

"No. I told him to email me when he made it back to Germany safely."

"What did he say?"

"He said he would. He actually emailed when he got in his seat on the airplane." I said.

"Brief conversation, huh?" Carrie asked.

"Yes I swear. Talking to him did come easy though, scary even." I said.

"Well he's all the way in the Germany." Carrie said.

An attractive man was walking up the sidewalk. Carrie lowered her sunglasses and said plenty of local fish to enjoy. We both laughed as the waiter placed our plates in front of us.

We continued chatting as we ate our lunch and enjoyed the beautiful weather. Strangely I was thinking about Bryson sitting with her. I couldn't remember how long he told me the flight was to Frankfurt. I looked up at the clouds in the sky and wondered what he was doing right now on his flight. Carrie snapped me out of my daydream.

"Sam! What store are we going to first?"

"Let's go to J Crew first then stop by White House Black Market." I said.

"Okay! I want to stop by the MAC store too before we leave." Carrie said.

"I need a new lip pencil." I said.

"You mean you want a new lip pencil." She laughed.

"No I really do."

"Sam, you can barely zip up your make up bag."

I laughed because she was telling the truth.

"You're right." I said.

We crossed Wisconsin Avenue and began our afternoon therapy. A lot of stores were offering sales for the new season. I thought about checking my phone to see if I had any new emails but decided not to. J Crew didn't have much so we quickly moved on. We weren't inside WHBM a New York minute before Carrie had grabbed two outfits and was inside a dressing room.

"Sam! Sam!"

She was standing at the entrance to the fitting room with one of the outfits on. I walked over to her. I didn't consider myself a jealous person but Carrie looked good in anything. Her body was shaped just right.

"What do you think Sam?" she asked.

She had on a coral pencil skirt and a white blouse with a ruffled collar with a one button blazer.

"You look great girl! I love that color on you." I said.

"I think I could go a size smaller in the blouse."

I came closer and opened the blazer to see how the blouse was fitting.

"I think it looks fine." I said.

"My boobs feel huge. My period is about to start." She whispered and laughed.

"Girl you are a mess." I said.

She turned and headed back inside the fitting room. I continued looking for something for myself. I wanted a new dress but I didn't like the selection they had in stock. I did see a nice yellow off the shoulder dress. They had it paired with a brown strap wedge. I took a size 6 and 8 to try on. When I got to the fitting room, Carrie had on a pair of blue patterned capris with a light colored shell top. She spun around slowly like she was on the runway in Paris.

"What do you think Sam?" She asked.

"You want the truth?" I smiled.

"Yes!" She frowned.

"I love the capris but you could lose the top."

"I wasn't really feeling the top either. Thanks girl." She said. "I love that color yellow on you by the way."

"Thank you! Let's see which size fits better." I laughed.

I could wear some 6s but my rear end sometimes forced me into an 8. Then I'd have to get the waist taken in. Thanks momma for the curves and thanks dad for no waistline. I couldn't get the dress zipped up fast enough.

"How does the 6 fit Sam?" Carrie asked.

I didn't need everyone in the fitting room knowing my size.

"Shhh! Carrie, give me a minute."

I opened the door and Carrie was standing there waiting for me.

"Sam you look beautiful. Which one is this?" She asked.

"It's the 6?" I said.

"The running is paying off."

"Yeah I guess. I thought I needed an 8.

"No you don't! This is a great fit on you." She said. "Are you going to buy it?"

I looked at myself in the long mirror and then turned to the side. I had to admit I like the way I looked in the dress.

"Oh come on Sam, when's the last time you bought yourself anything?" She asked.

"The last time we went shopping in Annapolis." I said.

"Oh! Yes you did. Still you should get that dress?" Carrie said.

I walked back into my fitting room and unzipped the dress. I looked at it hanging up and it did look nice. I began getting dressed and I heard my phone beep twice. It was an email from my work account. I quickly pulled my cell phone from my purse to check the email. It was just a server maintenance alert. When I came out of the fitting room I saw Carrie at the register paying for what she tried on minus the shell top that we both didn't like. I was still undecided about the dress. I walked slowly towards the rack it was hanging on, looking it up and down. Carrie turned around and saw me walking. In a low to medium voice she yelled, "Get it Sam. It looks great on you." I stopped and held the dress away from me playing scenarios of why I should and why I shouldn't get the dress. I pulled on it, then pressed it against the front of my body and lifted one of my legs. Okay I'll get it. Worse case I'll keep the receipt.

When I got to the register the person checking me out told me she had a 40% coupon and applied it to the total for me. I guess it was meant for me to buy the dress after all. I paid for the dress and walked out of the store where Carrie was on her phone waiting.

"Sam I'm glad you bought the dress."

"The lady at the counter applied a 40% coupon for me."

"That was nice of her. Where to next?" Carrie asked.

Before I could answer I heard my cell phone beep again, probably another maintenance alert. I ignored it as we headed to the MAC store.

"How's Jonathan doing?" I asked.

"That wasn't Jonathan!" She said.

"Stop lying. Who else would you tell 'bye love' to?" I laughed.

"I call my mother that all of the time."

"Was that your mother?" I asked.

She held a straight face for as long as she could.

"No girl. It was Jonathan." She laughed.

We stood there laughing like high school girls that had a crush on the star athlete. I was happy that Carrie found someone that made her happy. The last relationship was a complete disaster. Barry could cook with the best of them. But when he got high he was another person. That person began abusing Carrie. If she hadn't left that relationship we probably wouldn't be standing here laughing.

"I'm glad you found someone that makes you happy Carrie."

"Me too but I'm not singing wedding jingles just yet."

"Every kiss begins K!" I sang.

"Oh stop it girl." She said. "We have to find you someone now."

"It will happen when it's meant to."

We grabbed hands and walked towards the other shops looking at the window mannequin displays. As we walked into the MAC store my cell phone beeped twice. I pulled it out and checked it this time. It was an email from Bryson. The subject line read – *I'm back safely*. There was nothing else in the body of the email. Carrie had walked ahead and was browsing the eyeliners. I hit the reply button, but I wasn't sure how to respond. I guess I was hoping for more than three words. A MAC rep walked up to me and asked if he could help me. I quickly typed *Thanks* and hit send and told the MAC rep I was looking for the amber times 9-palette eye shadow, a velvet teddy lipstick and a subculture lip liner.

Chapter 6

Carrie and I finished at the MAC store and ended our day with a stop by Victoria's Secret. The sun was starting to set, and a different vibe was coming alive on Wisconsin Avenue. The sought-after Civil Cigar Lounge line was beginning to fill up and local pubs and bars were lined with mini-skirts and high heels.

"I'm glad we got a chance to hang out Sam."

I hugged Carrie and told her I had a great time as well and let's do it again sometime soon. We kissed each other's cheek and said our goodbyes. I turned and walked to my car. I pulled out my cell phone to check my parking meter app to make sure my time hadn't expired. I had a text message from Trent.

Hi Sam! I hope you're doing well.

I didn't reply. It was no need to give him any hope of us becoming more than friends. I called my parents to see what they were doing. My mom answered laughing loudly.

"Hunt residence! Who's speaking?" she asked.

"It sounds like you guys are having a party," I said.

"Hi, Sam! No. Your father and I were looking at some old pictures of us in college," she said. "What are you doing?"

"Oh okay. I spent the afternoon with Carrie. I was going to stop by."

"We'll see you when you get here baby," she said before hanging up.

My parents were still in love with each other after 40 years of marriage. They met when they were both attending Sam Houston State University. My mother was from Texas, but my father was from Arizona. They majored in international business and pursued MBAs at the same school before moving to the DC area. The story is, they met through mutual friends but didn't like each other initially. My mom says my dad pursued her. But my dad's side of the story is, she disguised her attraction to him by asking a random question about accounting and then asking if they could study together sometime. Who knows what memories those two were laughing at when I called? They bought a home in Upper Marlboro, Maryland shortly after they moved to the Nation's Capital. They retired a few years ago from one of the top international accounting firms in DC.

I turned the volume up on the Sirius station playing and took the 495 beltway towards Maryland. Carrie called me and told me she was home and how much fun she had again. I told her it was a great afternoon and I look forward to doing it again soon. Traffic was the typical flow for a Saturday evening. An unknown caller appeared on my dash screen. I didn't normally receive those kinds of calls. I wonder if it was Trent reaching out in a desperate way. I let the call keep ringing until it went to voicemail. I continued driving and waited to see if the unknown caller would leave a message. After a few minutes, I didn't receive a voicemail indicator on my screen. The DJ on Sirius was playing all of Jill Scott's hits. *Is this the way* played loudly through my speakers. I was shaking my head to the beat and singing in my best American Idol's voice. I loved Jill Scott's voice. Her songs spoke to me, past relationships and my soul. A few more of her greats came on. I was just about to the exit for my parent's house when I received another call from an unknown caller. I answered in an annoyed voice because I truly was.

"Ms. Hunt speaking."

"Hi, Samantha. It's Bryson."

I pressed on the brakes to slow my speed. I looked at the clock in my car and tried to calculate what time it was in Germany – 2:17 AM. Then my thoughts went to the three-word email. He called my name again.

"Hi, Bryson."

"Did I catch you at a bad time?" he asked.

"What time is it over there?" I already knew.

"It's a little after two in the morning."

"Jetlagged?" I asked.

"Not really. I needed to call and apologize to you," he said.

"For what?"

"My email."

"I asked you to email me when you made it back. You did that," I said.

"I wanted to say so much more though."

"I'm sure you were tired after the flight."

"No, I wasn't. After I hung up with you, I had a disturbing voicemail from my ex-girlfriend."

I was coming up on the exit for my parents' house, and I wasn't sure what to say.

"Is everything okay?" I asked.

"Yes!" he said sternly.

"Really? What happened?"

"She was upset I didn't make an effort to see her while I was in the states," he said.

I was close to the street that my parents lived on. I pulled over.

"I'm sorry to hear that," I said, "why didn't you see her?"

My mom was calling on the other line.

"Bryson, I need to take this call. Can you hold on or we can just talk later?"

"I can hold on," he said. I clicked over and told my mom I was close but needed to finish up a call from work. She said,

Okay and get there safely." I had never lied to my mother, but I didn't want to get into who Bryson was and how we met.

"Okay sorry about that."

"No problem."

"Do you still love her?"

"Yes I do but sometimes love isn't enough."

"Love should always be enough," I said.

"You're right! If the love is mutual," he said.

"She didn't love you?" I asked.

"That was one of our challenges."

"How so?"

"She held on to the hurt from her previous relationship."

"Yes, I agree that is a challenge."

"I was becoming tired of being in competition with her past."

"So who ended the relationship?"

"She did."

"How long ago?"

"Seven months."

It had been a while since the breakup, so I wasn't sure why a voicemail would have him so upset.

"Samantha, this isn't the first time something like this has happened."

I didn't know him well enough to know all the details of his relationship, and I probably had already asked too many questions, so I remained quiet. Besides, it was time for me to get to my parents' house.

"Bryson I'm sorry to cut you off. I was on my way to my parents' house when you called. My mom called while you and I were talking. I should get there so they're not worried."

"No problem. Sorry for keeping you so long," he said.

"You should get some rest. Do you work Monday?" I asked.

"Yes!"

"Oh, okay."

"Enjoy your visit with your parents."

"Are you going to be okay?"

He laughed. I sensed a bit of stubbornness.

"Yes, I'm much better now."

"Okay, Mr. Garrison!"

"Please. Call me Bryson."

"Okay, Bryson." I laughed.

"Thanks for listening when you didn't have to," he said.

"No problem," I said.

"Enjoy the rest of your weekend."

"You do the same."

"Take care, Samantha."

"You can call me Sam. Email me sometime," I said.

"I will do that."

"Goodbye Bryson."

He didn't say goodbye, I just heard the line go dead. I turned into my parents' driveway, and the bright motion light from their porch came on. Then I saw the front door open, and my dad walked out onto the porch. He did this every time I came home to visit. My father undoubtedly was the first man I ever fell in love with, and I'm hopeful there's at least one more man in this world that I will fall in love with again. I got out of my car and walked towards my dad. When I reached the porch, he outstretched his arms and hugged me.

"So good to see you Sam!" he said.

He always made me feel welcome to come home. My mom had come out onto the porch. I felt her hand touch mine then she patted my dad's shoulders. I wanted the kind of love my parents had – that soul burning, can't breathe without you love I heard in song lyrics. My dad stopped hugging me and grabbed my mother's hand and mine before walking back into the house.

Pictures of me from my childhood were still on the walls and pieces of furniture along with pictures of my parents through the years from various trips. I thought about Bryson and how he must be feeling in Germany alone and silently wished for him to be happy and have what I see in my parents. I stayed at my parents a few hours talking and laughing with them. We talked about the family reunions we'd gone to on both sides of the families. Of course, the question came up about my dating life and when I was going to give them some grandkids. That wasn't in the cards any time soon for me, and I knew that saddened them. But their smiles remained, and they told me when God's ready for it to happen, then it will, don't mind them. I believed in God, and I also knew my parents were getting up there in age. I wondered if they regretted having only one child while pursuing their careers? When the subject of grandkids came up, it was always plural. I stayed a little while longer. It was getting late, and my parents still went to bed at a particular time no matter what.

When I got home, I took a long hot bath and let my body relax from the day. I had the sounds of John Coltrane playing, and Max was sitting by the bathroom door. I finished my bath and fell asleep in no time.

Chapter 7

I woke up Sunday morning from a great night of sleep. I decided to skip my run and attend the early morning church service. My Sundays consisted of church, lifetime movies, and light chores. I picked out a black dress, put on a little makeup, and curled my hair before I got dressed. I changed Max's litter box before heading out. I was a member of the Way of Faith Christian Center in Silver Springs, Maryland. The pastor was in his early 40s and full of Godly praise. The congregation was a mix of all walks of life, and I enjoyed the message.

As I was pulling into the parking lot, Carrie texted me.

"Do you have any plans today?" she asked.

"My usual Sunday routine. Why?"

"I wanted to come over this afternoon."

"Is something wrong?" I asked.

"No. I just wanted to see you again."

"Okay. I'm parking at my church. I'll call you after the service," I said.

"Okay, Sam. Say a prayer for me."

"I always do," I told her.

I parked in the spot chosen by the parking attendant and sat with a puzzled look on my face. Carrie knew how I spent my Sundays, so it was odd to hear her ask to come over. I walked into my church building speaking to everyone as I made my way to my usual seat – 6 rows from the front. I silenced my phone and pulled out my Bible to receive today's word.

    The pastor's message was simple yet powerful. *If you're going to pray about it, don't worry about it.* He said, "Leave it in God's hand instead of stressing about it." I sat there enjoying his message and thinking about my best friend. I headed to the grocery store to pick up a few things to make dinner and my lunch for the coming week. I made it back to my side of town in no time. The weather was still nice, and people were out jogging, walking their dogs, and pushing strollers or walking with their toddlers. The outside patios of the coffee bean houses and restaurants were filled with patrons.

    I walked into the market with the list I had written in the parking lot and grabbed a small cart. My mom always told me to shop the outer lanes of the market. I did the best I could but occasionally went down a few of the center aisles. I loved my carbs. I picked up a couple of bags of salad mix, fruit, and some fresh vegetables. I picked up some deli meat for my lunch the coming week and fat-free milk before heading to the checkout.

    As I loaded my groceries into my car, my cell phone beeped three times indicating I had three voicemails. I finished putting my recyclable bags in the backseat then checked them. The first message was from my parents saying hello and inviting me over for Sunday dinner if I was interested. The next message was from a telemarketer soliciting me to get paid to do online shopping or something. I deleted the message before it finished. The last message was a ghost from my past – William Henry Randolph. This man held my heart like clay in his hands for years. I used to change my bed sheets weeks after his body laid on them. We were engaged to be married but he fell deeper in love with his career, and our wedding date kept getting farther and farther until I ended it.

Hi Sam! It's Will, I hope you're doing well. I'll be in DC this week for a business meeting and was wondering if we could have dinner. My number is still the same. I hope to hear from you.

His voice was still the same; mesmerizing and heart melting. I sat in my parking lot replaying his voicemail and thinking if I should even return his phone call. We hadn't physically spoken since last Christmas. I sent him a text for his birthday, but that had been the extent of our conversation. I started my car and headed home to get ready for the week. I called Carrie back.

"Hi, Sam! How was the service?" she asked.

"Carrie it was the spiritual feeding I needed," I said. "You should have come."

"I know. I was being lazy," she said.

"I prayed for you anyway."

"Thank you," she said.

"Guess who called me?"

"Brian," she said laughing.

"I don't know anyone named Brian," I said, "do you mean Bryson?"

"Yes, him."

"No! William," I said.

"What did that creep want?" Her attitude was evident.

"Carrie, that's not nice," I said. "He's not a bad guy."

"Okay! What did he want Sam?"

"He's going to be here this week and wants to have dinner."

"Did you tell him you're busy the rest of the year?" she asked.

I laughed. Carrie was by my side during the breakup. She sat on my couch with me and shared many spoons of butter pecan ice cream and watched more than her fair share of Sunday Lifetime movies with me.

Then helped me shed the 20 pounds I gained. She was truly my best friend.

"He left a voicemail," I said, "I didn't speak to him."

"Good! Don't return the call. He'll assume you're busy," she said.

"I haven't decided yet," I said.

"Sam! What could you two possibly have to talk about?"

"Carrie it's just dinner."

"Okay, let's have dinner this week," she said.

"Sure, what night?"

"Whatever night William wants to have dinner," she said and laughed.

"You're hilarious Carrie," I said.

"Oh goodness! You're considering it aren't you?" she asked.

She knew me all too well. I was actually. Just listening to his voice made me think about his Colgate smile, his manly hands, the insatiable love we used to make, and those green eyes were romantically charming. I used to love this man like no other. My dad was the first man I fell in love with, and William was certainly the second.

"Carrie I'm pulling up to my condo garage. I'll call you back when I get inside."

"Okay! Call me back *before* you make your dinner plans," she said.

"Bye Carrie!"

I walked in, and Max greeted me at the door. I put up my groceries and then sat on my couch and rubbed him still thinking about the last voicemail I received from William. Then I thought about all I went through with William and the happy place I was now in. Could I survive his charm and get through the evening without ending up back in his hotel room or him in my condo.

"Hi, Sam!" he said.

My heart started the meltdown countdown.

"Hi William, how are you? I got your voicemail," I said sternly.

"I'm well. How are you?" he asked.

"I'm well. Why are you coming to DC?"

"I'm meeting some investors. Are you busy?"

I wasn't ready to answer his invitation.

"That's good. What property are you looking to buy now?" I asked.

"There's a huge parcel in southern Maryland that I'm thinking about going in on with them."

"Oh, I see," I said.

The silence on the line was uncomfortable for both of us.

"Sam! I know it's been a while. I was just hoping to see you. I miss you."

"I wish you all the best with your meeting, but I don't think having dinner is a good idea," I said.

He didn't say anything. The silence was fighting back.

"William I should go. Good luck with your meeting."

"Sam, will you at least think about it?" he asked.

I could hear the sense of defeat in his voice. Once upon a time he could have asked me to meet him anywhere, and I'd drop everything I was doing to be there. For years, William was a priority in my life, but in the end, he made me feel like I was only an option in his. He moved to New York so quickly after our break up leaving me to deal with everything.

"Bye William."

I called my parents back to let them know I wasn't coming over and relaxed the rest of the day. I'm sure my first day back in the office was going to be busy.

Chapter 8

I had only been in the office a few minutes before my supervisor called me to her office. I locked my computer screen and proceeded to her office.

"Good morning Sam!"

"Good morning," I said.

"Did you see the emails about the server upgrade?" she asked.

"I did," I said, "why do you ask?"

"I want you to oversee it and let me know if there are any issues."

"Ma'am! I had planned to work on my report from the conference."

"Oh, that can wait. This is a priority," She said.

"Okay. Is there anything else?" I asked.

"No, that will be all. Thanks, Sam."

I stood up to leave her office, and as I reached her door, I heard her say, "This upgrade will get us up to speed like our team in Germany."

I turned around and smiled as I exited.

When I got back to my desk, I called the IT section to find out what time was the upgrade set to begin. They confirmed it would start at 10 o'clock this morning and that the system will be slower but other than that all should go smoothly. I thanked them and started reading the emails I needed to reply to and deleted the ones taking up space in my inbox. My desk phone interrupted my deleting efforts. The caller ID read DHS-C-DE. I didn't recognize the office symbol.

"Hi, this is Samantha Hunt!"

"Good morning Ms. Hunt!"

I didn't expect to hear from Bryson so soon. I looked at the clock display on my phone to see what time it was over there.

"Hi, Bryson. You should be getting off soon right?" I asked.

"I never leave at the exact time I should."

"Is your team busy over there?" I asked.

"No more than normal. I always stayed later than everyone else."

"Oh okay," I said. "What do you normally do in the evening over there?"

"I normally hit the local gym and head home if I don't have any other plans," he said.

"Do you get normal TV over there?" I asked.

"Define normal." He laughed.

"Do you get the TV shows we get in the states? What about sports?"

"Yes, but they're a few weeks behind. Yes, we get live sports, but with the time difference it's hard to catch it." He laughed.

"I can see how that would be tough," I said.

"We do okay over there though."

The playful banter between us went on for a few more minutes, and the comfort level of the conversation was again surprising to both of us. I looked at the digital display on my phone, and we had been talking for over thirty minutes.

"Bryson, I'm not a director, so I need to get back to work."

"Oh goodness! Where does the time go? We've been on the phone quite a while," he said.

"Yes, we have. Enjoy your evening."

"Enjoy your Monday Sam."

"One second, I have another call," I said.

Ms. Hunt, this is the security desk, you have a delivery.

"I'm back Bryson. I have to go. That was the front desk security. I have a package."

"Nice talking to you Sam."

"Likewise," I said.

We hung up, and I walked to the elevators and down to the front desk security. I wasn't expecting anything, so I was more than curious about the delivery.

When I stepped off the elevator, I saw a vase with a bouquet of yellow roses for someone on the counter.

"Good morning guys," I said.

"Good morning Ms. Hunt. The flowers are for you," one of the guards said.

"This must be some sort of mistake," I said.

The guard showed me the sign-in log. A delivery person signed the sign-in log; reason for visit said delivery to Samantha Hunt. Before I reached for the white envelope I thought to myself – *William was still charming and was trying hard to get me to dinner.* I pulled the note card from the envelope, and as I read the note my heart stopped, and I felt myself blushing.

Hi Sam, it's Bryson. I wanted to wish you a happy week and thank you for listening to me the other day. Take care and until the next time. BG.

I felt the security guards looking at me and wondering what the card said that had me visibly smiling. I thanked them and got back on the elevator. I hadn't received flowers since I was in a relationship with William. It felt a little weird especially from someone fresh out of a relationship; at least they're yellow and not red. I didn't have the authority to make international phone calls so I would send Bryson an email to thank him. When I got to my floor, I tried to rush back to my cubicle hoping no one would see the roses. I know if anyone saw them, the gossiping would start since I hadn't spoken of a relationship in at least two years. No one in my office knew about Trent. I didn't see the point because I wasn't in an exclusive relationship with him. I made it to my cubicle without running into anyone. Or at least I thought I did.

"So, who's the lucky guy?" Donovan asked.

I smiled but didn't answer. Donovan had been asking me out for the longest time. Although he was handsome and appeared to be very nice, I kindly kept turning him down. I had seen my share of office romances go awry. He left my cubicle and I unlocked my computer screen to email the sender of the flowers, but I already had an email from him. The message was an extension of the 100 characters allowed for delivery messages. I hit the reply button and said 'call me please.' Within a few minutes, my desk phone started ringing with the same caller ID from earlier.

"Hello, Mister!" I said with a smile.

"No office greeting?" he asked."

"Thank you. You shouldn't have," I said.

"You're welcome."

"I'm thankful Bryson. It's just that..."

"It's just that what?" he asked.

"It's barely been 48 hours since we met," I said, "you didn't have to send me flowers."

"I really appreciate you listening to me," he said.

"You told me thank you on the phone," I said, looking at the flowers.

"Do you at least like them?" he asked, ignoring me.
"They're beautiful!" I said.
"Great! You never know how online deliveries will turn out."
"Bryson!"
"Yeah, Sam!"
"What are we doing here?"
"Having a casual conversation after you've received your first delivery from me," he said.
"First?" I asked.
"You know what I mean Sam."
"Okay," I said.

I held the phone looking at the beautiful flowers and at the same time trying to make some sense of this happening so fast.

"Bryson I'm very thankful for your gesture, but I think you're feeling vulnerable."

"I know what I'm feeling," he said. "Talking to you came easier than I ever imagined and I'm thankful."

"Okay, I won't take it for anything more," I said.

I told Bryson thank you again and told him I really needed to get back to work and that he should leave his office as well. Before hanging up, he apologized for being so forward. I told him it was fine. Then he asked me a personal question.

"Sam! When is your birthday?"

I wasn't sure I wanted to answer him. Until now the conversation had been about the department and *his past* relationship. My tongue felt otherwise as the date rolled off easily.

"January 16th," I said.
"Thank you! Bye Sam."
"Yours?" I asked.
"June 16th."

"Your big day is coming up," I said.
"Yes, it is."
"Any big plans?" I asked.
"None yet."
I hadn't realized it, but the conversation had continued after we were supposed to hang up minutes ago.
"Bryson I really have to go. Enjoy your evening."
"Have a great day," he said.
We finally hung up, but the international call could have gone on longer. I looked at the flowers again and smiled. I needed to call Carrie first chance I got. I checked on the progress of the server upgrade. The IT team told me it was moving smoothly. I told them I'd check back with them after lunch.
I finished my salad with cucumbers, tomatoes, chopped eggs, grilled chicken breasts, and red onions then I called Carrie. She answered loud and laughing.
"What's so funny?" I asked.
"Hi, Sam!" she said. "I'm watching Jack Nicholson in As Good As It Gets."
"What part?"
"It just started. He's washing his hands in scalding hot water and then throwing away the soap."
I joined in the laughter with Carrie. That was good movie.
"How's it going, Sam?" she asked.
"I received flowers today."
I heard the background noise go silent and Carrie moving around.
"From who?" she asked, "William?"
"No!"
"Trent?" she asked.
"No! Bryson," I said.

"The guy from the conference?"
"Yes."
"Why?" she asked.
"He wanted to thank me for listening to him."
"Wow! Should I call Oprah or Dr. Phil?" She laughed.
"Stop it, Carrie."
"Seriously Sam. You've had two conversations with this man," she said.
"I know. The flowers are yellow."
"Are you trying to be funny?" she asked.
"No, I'm just saying."
"Saying what? He's less creepy?" she asked.
"I have everything under control," I said.
"Are you sure?" she sounded concerned.
"Yes, Carrie," I said. "And why are you off today?"
"I needed a mental day." She laughed.
"I could have used a day off, but I needed to come in," I said.
"Yes, and you would've missed your delivery." She laughed.
"You're hilarious," I said.
"Have you heard back from William?" she asked.
Nice way to change the subject.
"No, I haven't."
"*When* you do, remember you're busy the rest of the year," she said.
"You're too funny," I said.
"Okay, Sam I'm going back to Jack."
"Enjoy, and I'll talk to you soon."

Carrie and I hung up, and I finished up my day in the office. I sent an email to my supervisor informing her the server upgrade was complete with no issues. She quickly replied and thanked me and told me to have a good evening.

Chapter 9

I left the office and entered the evening traffic headed home. I turned on my radio and listened to Sirius Heart and Soul. Chante Moore's candlelight and you was playing. I thought about my life and admitted for the first time in a long time that I was lonely. I missed affection, companionship, male-female communication, and caring for another person. I continued up Constitution Ave and Rachelle Ferrell's nothing has ever felt like this came on the station. Her song lyrics spoke to my soul and gave me chills yearning for endearing love. I needed to talk to my dad.

"Hi, baby girl! How was your day?" he asked.

"It was full of surprises," I said.

"Most Mondays are."

"Dad where's mom?"

"I think she's getting some laundry out of the dryer," he said. "Do you need to speak with her?"

"Oh no, I was just asking," I said. "Can I ask you a question?"

"Of course. What's on your mind baby?"

For as long as I could remember, my dad always had a calming demeanor and was ready to talk about anything with me – good or bad.

"When did you know you wanted to date mom?" I asked.

"The minute she said hello!" he said.

"When did you propose?" I asked.

"In my mind shortly after hello," he said. "Our senior year of undergrad."

I didn't say anything.

"Baby girl, is this about William?" he asked.

"No, why did you bring him up?"

"I haven't heard you talk about marriage since you and him broke off the engagement."

"I'm sorry for snapping at you dad."

"It's okay. Love is a delicate subject with you young folks these days." He laughed.

"People play so many games," I said. "I don't have the energy."

"The right man will appreciate you," he said.

"He better!" I said.

"Something you want to tell me, Sam?" he asked, "is this about Trent?"

My dad knew me too well. He could sense my moods from the beginning of the conversation.

"No. I met a guy at the conference."

"Okay."

"He sent me flowers already," I said.

"He sounds like a gentlemen Sam."

"He works for the agency," I said.

"You know it's not good mixing business and pleasure."

"He doesn't live in DC dad."

"Where does he live?" he asked.

I heard the fatherly stern voice.

"Germany"

"Oh, I see," he said. "Do you like him?"

"He's all the way in Germany," I said.

"That wasn't my question Sam."

"I don't know dad, but he is nice and talking to him came so easy."

"Well, you need to decide if you like him first," he said.

"I'm so afraid these days," I said.

"You don't even know if you like him."

My dad was an intelligent man. He was just going along with me to appease me. He already knew I liked Bryson.

"I've heard the nightmares of long distance relationships," I said.

"Sam! Relationships are work regardless if it's local or long distance," he said.

"How did you and mom make it work in college?"

"Your mother was all about her grades," he said. "She wasn't worried about me or any other college knucklehead."

"So how did you guys start dating."

"Hard work and persistence my dear," he said.

"Thank you, Dad."

"Anytime Sam," he said. "What's his name?"

"Bryson."

"One last thing Sam; don't worry about what others think," he said.

By now I was crying listening to my dad's words of wisdom. I did struggle with what others thought. I overanalyzed a lot of things. He heard my sniffles.

"Sam it's going to be fine. Trust your heart," he said.

I wiped the slow stream of tears and asked him if I could speak to mom. Before he gave her the phone, he told me his famous quote, 'You can't cheat love.'

"Hey, Sam! How are you doing?" she asked.

"I'm well mom and you?"

"Just cleaning up a bit and about to have dinner with your father."

"What's for dinner?" I asked.

"I made a meatloaf, green beans, and mashed potatoes."

"Sounds good. You guys enjoy. I love you."

"We love you too. What were you and your father talking about?" she asked.

My mother was just as smart as my dad and probably heard his responses and knew something was going on with me.

"Aww, mom. Dad-daughter stuff," I said laughing.

"Are you okay Sam?" she asked.

"Never better mom," I said, "I'll talk to you guys later on in the week."

"Good night Sam!"

"Good night mom!"

As I pulled into my parking garage, William was calling. I had this thing about not deleting numbers from my phone. I didn't answer his call and continued inside the garage. When I got off the elevator, my phone beeped, and the voicemail icon appeared on my screen. I unlocked my door while the message played.

Hi Sam! It's Will! I'm in DC. I hope you've reconsidered. I'm at the Ritz in Northwest, and you have my cell. Talk to you soon.

I deleted Will's message and bent down to rub Max. I jumped in the shower and thought about Bryson and my dad's advice. After my shower, I started watching an episode of Grey's Anatomy.

Chapter 10

I woke up in a familiar yet displeasing place – William's hotel room. I had called his room from the hotel lobby shortly after 10 PM. The battle of love and lust was beating me down like I was in a professional boxing match with no training. I rationalized with myself that I would get some loving and ask for forgiveness later. Hell, men did it all of the time without regard.

"Mr. Randolph, you have a guest," the concierge said then handed me the phone. In a soft squeamish voice, I said, "It's me!"

"Sam!"

"Yes."

I could hear him grinning like the big bad wolf in little red riding hood.

"I'm in room 1210."

I handed the phone back to the concierge, and I heard him tell William he'd put me on an elevator. The ride up seemed like forever confirming what I knew; that I shouldn't be here. I heard the elevator ding on the 12th floor. When the doors opened, William was standing there with sweats and a tank top on. His body physique was still beautifully muscular, and he looked as handsome as ever. He greeted me with a smile.

"How are you, Sam?"

I couldn't even make eye contact with him, but I mustered up a response.

"I'm well William."

I didn't ask how he was. I stepped off the elevator, and he reached for my hand, but I resisted.

"It's okay Sam. I'm just glad to see you."

"Are you really?"

"Of course I am."

He was always happy to see and also happier to be rid of me with no commitment just some casual sex from his ex-fiancé. I continued to give him the best of both worlds, shame on me.

His room was a suite as usual. I could tell he was working before my lustful intentions interrupted him.

"Would you like a glass of wine Sam? I have a French Merlot one of my clients gave me."

He knew I loved red wine.

"Sure, I'll have a glass. What were you working on?" I asked.

I watched him walk to the kitchen. Everything about him still turned me into PlayDoh.

"I was looking over the layout of the property I told you about."

"Does it look like a profitable deal?"

"I'm still running the numbers. Charles County is a thriving county."

"Yes, I've heard that. It's still too far for me though."

"That's one of the cons I'm considering."

He returned with my glass of wine. He had a glass as well. Time stopped as we looked at each other with our glasses. Normally two people would make a toast. There was nothing normal about us.

"Thank you," I said.

"You're welcome."

His soul piercing eyes were looking right at me, and his smile was mesmerizing.

"Sam if you don't mind I need to finish looking over this layout."

Absolutely nothing had changed with him. What are you doing here Samantha?

"Sure, no problem. Mind if I turn the TV on?" I asked.

"The one in bedroom please."

I should have finished my wine and left.

"Okay," I said.

I sat in the bedroom watching TV and occasionally looking at him. It wasn't much longer before he came to the bedroom.

"I need to shower. Would you care to join me?" he asked.

He was really acting as if we hadn't skipped a beat.

"No thank you," I said.

He pulled off his tank top in front of me displaying his chocolate muscular chest. His body had very little fat on it, his abs were tight, and his shoulders were broader than I remember. I quietly exhaled and bit my bottom lip. When he turned to walk to the bathroom, I saw the definition on his back. I heard the shower water and visualized him taking his sweats off and revealing his buns of steel.

I heard the shower water stop, and William appeared with a pair of shorts on. He came over to the chair I was sitting in and knelt down in front of me.

"Sam, you're still beautiful as ever. Why did I disappoint you?"

"That's a good question. Why did you?"

"Selfish I suppose."

His honesty could be brutal at times. I had to appreciate that at least.

"Has anything changed?" I asked.

I knew the answer, but I enjoyed the pain of his honesty I guess.

"Oh, Sam. I just want to be successful." He smiled.

"At what cost though?"

His masculine hand touched the sides of my face. I felt my head lean into his hand.

"Sam I know I should have done things differently. But…"

"But what William?" I was getting upset.

He kissed me. He knew how to manipulate my emotions. I rendered to his soft kisses. He started to caress my shoulders. He was forming my body into the clay figure he needed it to be for the night. I felt him lifting my shirt over my head as he placed soft kisses on my body. I touched his body, and my hands went numb. He pushed me back onto the bed gently and rubbed his hands over my body. He softly caressed my breasts, and I heard a moan escape my mouth. Then I felt his strong hands in between my legs. I felt myself squirming and getting wet. He wasted no time sliding my pants off, but he left my panties on. Even after all of this time William still knew my body and how to turn me on. I felt his lips kiss the inside of my left thigh while his other hand slowly began rubbing the wet area in between my legs. More moans escaped my lips. He slid my panties off so slowly the anticipation was driving me insane. I was ready to feel him. He always took his time. When he stood up, I saw the joystick that had pleased me for years ready to continue the emotional damage. He slid his shorts off and climbed on top of me. He kissed my neck, then my right ear before sliding inside of me. I felt all of him fill me as my hands dug into his back. I felt his warm breath as he stroked me slowly and called my name.

"Sam you feel so good."

I didn't know how to respond. This wasn't our first time, but I wasn't exactly happy to be here. I remained silent as he continued softly speaking lies to me.

"I miss you so much."

He missed what we were doing right now. I closed my eyes and started asking for forgiveness.

"Come on Sam."

His strokes got faster and harder. I just couldn't get myself to express the pleasure I was receiving. The way he worked my body, I was sure to climax any minute now. He turned me over and slid back inside me. The penetration was deeper, and I climaxed quickly. I felt his grip around my hips tighten, and his penetrating thrusts became harder. I heard him whisper some vulgar words before saying I love you. William came. He laid next to me with his arm around me.

"Sam, can you ever forgive me?"

I didn't respond immediately.

"Sam, what if I moved back to DC? Could we try again?"

I was still laying there in silence and now confused.

"Are you serious?" I asked.

"Yes, I'm tired of being without you," he said.

"I don't believe you, William."

He squeezed my shoulders, then kissed the back of my neck.

"I am Sam. I really am."

I rested my hand on top of his hand and didn't respond to him. We fell asleep in that position.

I woke up to the smell of freshly brewed coffee. I hadn't expected to spend the night, so I had to get home and get ready for work. William came into the bedroom with a tray of fruit, an English muffin, juice, and a cup of coffee.

"Thank you, but I have to go," I said.

"Please have some breakfast," he said.

As much as I wanted to stay, it was time to go and time to stop doing this. In the heat of the moment, he mentioned moving back to

DC. I had heard it all before only to receive flowers and some empty rhetoric conversation.

"William, you and I both know this is as good as it gets."

I smiled and walked past him to the bathroom to get dressed. When I came out, he was sitting at the desk working. As I suspected, no more talk of moving back to DC or us getting back together. I walked over to the desk where William was working and kissed him on his right cheek.

"Sam! You don't have to go."

"I never should have been here."

I walked to the door and just before leaving I told him good luck.

Chapter 11

I drove home in complete silence. I showered and went to work. When I walked past the front desk security, one of the guys that were there when my flowers were delivered smiled at me. I smiled back and got in the elevator. When I walked into my office, I couldn't help but smile at the floral arrangement on my credenza. But I also felt terrible that I had gone to William's room. I logged on and immediately opened my email hoping to have an email from Bryson. I scanned my inbox but didn't have a new email from him. My cell phone started ringing. It was William. I didn't answer. I needed some hot tea. Before I headed to the cafeteria, I rechecked my email. The only emails I had received were software update reminders and meeting invites. I looked at my watch and then calculated what time it was in Germany. When I got to the cafeteria, I saw my supervisor getting coffee, and I tried to avoid her hoping she wouldn't see me.

"Good morning Ms. Hunt," she said.

"Morning."

"Great job with the server upgrade."

"I didn't do much. The IT team did the heavy lifting," I said.

"You're so selfless," she said.

"Well, I need to get in line to get some tea so I can get back to my office," I said.

"Very well. I'll stop by later this morning," she said before walking off.

"I'll be there."

She turned and walked off speaking to everyone coming into the cafeteria. She was a bubbly lady always in great spirits. I paid for my medium tea and headed back to my office.

When I logged back into my computer, there was a high priority email about a possible breach at our Dallas site. I could hear several conversations going on outside my office. Everyone was on their computers typing and on their phones inquiring about the breach. Just then my supervisor called me as well.

"Yes, Ma'am?" I asked.

"Have you heard about the breach in Dallas?" she asked.

"Yes I saw it," I said. "Do you know how much information has been stolen?"

"The damage is still being assessed."

"Have they at least been able to stop the hack?" I asked.

"They're working diligently but whoever did this knew how to penetrate around our firewall protection."

"Let me know if I can do anything," I said.

"Stand by Sam."

I sat there the rest of the morning reading the incoming email reports on the hack in Dallas. My supervisor called me again.

"Sam do you have lunch plans?" she asked.

I could tell the way she asked the question, she had made lunch plans for me. I started to fib and say yes.

"No I don't," I said hesitantly.

"Great! Meet me in the cafeteria at noon. We need to talk about the hack today and you possibly going to Dallas," she said before hanging up.

The rest of my morning was consumed with the news from Dallas. Just before noon, I promptly headed down to the cafeteria to meet my supervisor. When I arrived, the area was crowded and loud with much of the same news from earlier. I stood in line to order a tuna melt on wheat. I saw Ms. Cooper walk in and she spotted me in line. She had her lunch with her and pointed to a corner table. I nodded my head and waved my hand to acknowledge where she was sitting. I paid for my sandwich, yogurt, and sparkling water then headed over to where Ms. Cooper was seated.

"That looks good Sam," she said.

"It's a tuna melt. Would you like half?" I asked.

"No, thank you. I have a salad."

I sat down and prepared to hear my fate. I had just gotten back from the conference and really wasn't ready to leave again. Ms. Cooper had her head bowed blessing her food. When she finished, she wasted no time getting to business.

"So Sam, as you know our Dallas office was hacked this morning," she said as she took a bite of her salad.

I had already taken a bite of my sandwich.

"You mentioned me possibly going to Dallas," I said.

She took two more bites of her salad and wiped her mouth before responding.

"Yes! I thought of you first to go out and help the recovery team," she said.

I was grateful for the high regard, but I really didn't want to go.

"Thank you Ms. Cooper. When would I have to leave?" I asked.

"As soon as possible. Is there a problem?" she asked.

"Not at all. I'm asking because I would have to make arrangements for my cat."

"Oh yes. How could I forget? His name is Max, right?"

"Yes!"

"I should know more after the 2 o'clock staff meeting. I wanted to give you a heads up though," she said.

"I appreciate that."

"No problem Sam. You're one of if not the best in the office," she said.

We finished our lunch talking about how this hack really has the agency thinking of upgrading the systems to prevent this from happening again. We both stood to exit the cafeteria. When we walked onto the elevators, Ms. Cooper told me she'd reach out to me as soon as she hears something at the meeting. I pressed my floor button and she did the same. My desk phone was ringing as I walked back into my office. I didn't bother looking at the caller ID before answering.

"Hi, this is Sam."

"Hi there. I assumed you've been busy with the news from Dallas?"

His voice sounded so sexy even talking professionally. I stood there and exhaled.

"Hi Bryson," I said smiling.

"How are you Sam?"

"I'm well. I'm waiting to see if I have to go to Dallas," I told him.

"Oh okay. I wanted to call you before I dial into that meeting," he said, "I may have to come to Dallas as well."

"You could have called earlier." I pretended like I didn't hear the Dallas comment, but I was excited at an opportunity to possibly see him.

"I know but I wanted to call at this particular time," he said.

"What's so special about this time?" I asked.

"Look at the clock or your watch."

I looked at the clock on my office wall. The time was 1:16 in the afternoon.

"Okay, it's 1:16 in the afternoon," I said.

"Yes, it is. When I dialed your number, it was 1:16 your time."

It still wasn't registering with me.

"Sam, you told me your birthday was January 16th. So I will do my best to call you at the time whenever I call," he said.

Now I was blushing. No one had ever paid attention to details like this. A smile wide as the Potomac was on my face.

"Awww! Bryson, you're too cute. But you won't be at work this late all of the time," I said still smiling.

"Then I'll stop whatever I'm doing wherever I am and call," he said. "That is if you don't mind?"

"Of course not. But you know it's not necessary," I said.

"So they're saying the hackers were able to get close to 1 million identities from our system and maybe more," he told me.

"That's crazy. How can we recover from this?" I asked.

"Usually the hackers are looking for money."

I had never dealt with a hack since I had joined the agency so I wasn't sure how things were handled.

"Are you serious?" I asked, "do we normally pay what they're asking for?"

"We normally trace the computer and locate where the hack came from and send a team to the location as quickly as possible. Most times we're able to capture the criminals," he said.

"That sounds pretty serious," I said.

"I take it you've never dealt with a hack?" he asked.

"No! This is my first."

"Oh okay. Can I call you after the meeting Sam?"

"Sure, but you should get home. It's already late on that side of the world." I told him.

"I'm already home," he said.

I was blushing again.

"I'll talk to you after the meeting," I said.

"Thank you. Maybe we'll be in Dallas together," he said.

My goodness! This man sounded so good on the phone. I didn't really pay attention to it at the conference. His voice definitely has my attention now.

"We shall see. Talk to you soon Bryson."

"Until then," he said and hung up.

After hanging up with Bryson, I called my mom to let her know I may need her and my dad to check on Max. She answered on the third ring.

"Hi Sam! The news of a security hack in Dallas is all over the news," she said.

"Is it?" I asked.

"Yes honey. But anyway, how are you?" she asked.

"I'm well mom. I actually may have to go to Dallas," I said.

"You sound excited. Is this for the incident on the news?" she asked.

I didn't realize but I was still standing up and obviously blushing after speaking to Bryson.

"Yes mom it would pertain to what happened in Dallas," I said, "I'm waiting to hear after a 2 o'clock meeting."

"Well, don't worry about Max. Your dad and I will take care of him for you."

"Thanks, mom."

"Are you sure you're okay? I haven't heard you sound this happy in a long time," she said.

My mom could read me like a book with her eyes closed. I smiled and looked up at the clock before responding.

"Yes, mom I'm fine. Let me get back to work. Tell dad I said hello and I'll talk to you guys later once I hear about my trip."

"Okay dear. Enjoy the rest of your day."

"You too mom."

I sat down at my desk and logged back into my computer. There were more reports on Dallas and Carrie had emailed me to see if I was ok. She must have seen the news as well. My desk phone rang.

"Hi, Sam. Well, it looks like you don't have to go to Dallas after all. Enjoy the rest of your day," Ms. Cooper told me.

I slumped down in my chair, and my hand hit the desk slightly before I replied.

"Okay thank you, Ms. Cooper, for the update."

I wondered if Bryson had been told the same news. I tried to get some work done, but I was really waiting for his phone call. The next hour moved by slower than ever and I still hadn't heard back from him. I replied to Carrie's email and told her I was fine and that I thought I might have to go to Dallas but turns out I don't. I asked her what she was doing and let's meet for drinks maybe Thursday evening. She replied in minutes and confirmed Thursday for drinks at St. Eves. My desk phone rang while I was reading Carrie's response.

"Hi Sam! It's Bryson."

"Hey handsome." I couldn't believe I said that.

"Sorry I didn't call sooner. I had to book my flight and make my hotel reservations for Dallas," he said.

Bummer! He was going to Dallas, and I wasn't. My smile turned upside down.

"Oh okay. When do you leave?" I asked.

"Tomorrow morning. When do you leave?" he asked excitedly.

"I don't have to go Bryson."

The phone was silent for a few seconds.

"I was looking forward to seeing you again," he told me.

I could hear the change in his voice. We shared the same disappointment. I was sitting at my desk fidgeting with the phone cord and biting my bottom lip. I didn't know what to say.

"Sam!" he said.

"Yes, Bryson."

"Don't get mad but will you come to Dallas for the weekend? I'll buy your ticket."

"Bryson I'm flattered that you would ask me, but we've only talked a couple of times on the phone and-"

"I know, but I really don't want to come to the states and not see you."

"Let me think about it, and if I come, I'll get my own ticket," I told him.

"Sam not that I wouldn't be a gentleman, but I'll get you a separate room at the same hotel I'm staying in."

"Bryson you wouldn't have to do that. If I come to Dallas, then I trust you enough that you wouldn't do anything crazy."

"I appreciate that, and I hope you strongly consider coming," he said.

A ton of bricks fell on me right that moment. I felt like this was the same casual invite William offered me a few times when he'd come to DC for business. This sounded too familiar, and I wasn't going to be Bryson's stateside rebound romp in the sack. My frown stayed a little longer, and I became annoyed.

"Bryson I'll talk to you later," I said rudely.

"Is everything okay Sam?" he asked.

"Yes, I have to go."

"Are you sure?"

"Yes, good night!" I told him.

Even as rude as I sounded, he remained calm and showed what sounded like genuine concern about me.

"Goodbye, Sam."

I sat there looking at the phone and occasionally looking at the clock calculating what time it was on his side of the world. I opened the Internet browser and typed in www.expedia.com.

Chapter 12

I looked up the round trip airfare from DCA to DFW leaving this coming Friday and returning Sunday evening. The last-minute fares were $575.00 and up depending on the time of departure and return times. The cheaper fares had me getting in close to midnight on Friday evening and leaving at the crack of dawn on Sunday. I opened another travel site to make some comparisons but became frustrated with myself that I was even considering going. I logged off and headed home. I needed to meet my girl *before* Thursday.

"Hi, girl!" I yelled.

"Hey, Sam. Was your day stressful?" she asked.

"Not really. It didn't affect my location directly. Are you busy?" I asked bluntly.

"No. Jonathan is supposed to come by later," she said.

I had to remember Carrie had someone special and I couldn't just intrude on her in my time of need. I bit my bottom lip.

"What's wrong Sam?" she knew me too.

"I'm sorry I know you said Jonathan was coming by but can we meet for a few? I really need your advice," I pleaded.

"Of course we can. Jonathan has a key so I'll just tell him I may be a little late meeting him."

"When did Jonathan get a key?" I asked.

"Girl, not too long ago." She laughed.

"Oh I see." I was little annoyed.

Carrie's life was moving in the right directions it appeared and I was stuck barely over William and didn't want a relationship with Trent. Now Bryson's asking me to meet him in Dallas.

"So where would you like to meet?" she asked.

"I don't know it's Tuesday."

"How about McCormick's at the National Harbor?" she suggested.

"Okay, I'll head there."

"See you soon Sam."

I hung up with Carrie still thinking about Jonathan having a key to her place. Their relationship had gone to another level and Carrie hadn't told me. That seemed odd and not like Carrie. I called my mom back and told her I didn't have to go to Dallas and that I will see them later on in the week. I maneuvered as best as I could through the evening traffic in DC to meet Carrie. I was listening to the real sound of the DMV when my cell phone rang. The dashboard displayed an unknown caller. I quickly looked at the clock. It was after midnight and Bryson was calling me.

"Shouldn't you be asleep Mister?" I asked.

"I'm on my way but I was calling to see how you are feeling? You hung up so abruptly. I was concerned."

His sexy voice forced my smile to return.

"I apologize. I'm fine. I got distracted while talking to you and needed to refocus. That's all," I told him.

"Okay Sam. If you need to talk, you can call me anytime."

"I appreciate that. What time is your flight?"

"It's at 12:30 PM in the afternoon."

"Is it direct to Dallas?"

"Yes! Do you mind if I call you when I land on that side?" he asked.

"Sure no problem. Get some rest," I told him.

"I can sleep on the plane but okay I'll let you go."

"Safe travels handsome and I'll talk to you soon."

"Until then," he said before hanging up.

My smile remained all the way to the harbor. I parked and walked to McCormick's. A lot of people were out for it to be a Tuesday evening. I saw Carrie waiting out front for me with her cell phone up to her ear. She was always on the phone. I walked up to her, and she said her goodbyes to whomever, and we embraced and kissed each other's cheek like we always do.

"Sam did you see the two fine young men checking you out?"

"I wasn't paying attention."

"Well, you need to. One of them is really cute." She waved at them.

"Come on girl. Let's get inside," I told her.

"Do you want to sit at the bar or at a table? Inside or outside?" she asked me.

"Let's sit at a table outside if the wait isn't too long," I told her.

Carrie walked up to the hostess and asked for a table for two outside. I heard the hostess tell Carrie it would be about a fifteen-minute wait. Carrie looked at me, and I nodded that it was okay.

"So girl what's up? It must be serious if we're meeting on a Tuesday."

I wanted to ask more about the new living situation before we got into my issue.

"When the hack in Dallas happened, my supervisor told me I might have to go out there to help the recovery team. But after a meeting, she said I didn't have to go."

"Okay, so what's the problem?" Carrie asked.

The hostess called for us and said our table was ready. I didn't continue the conversation as we walked. I must admit I did see some nice looking men in the bar area as we walked through. I heard Carrie speaking as we made our way outside. The hostess sat us down and said our waiter would be with us shortly.

"Okay, Sam you were saying you didn't have to go to Dallas."

"Yes, I don't have to go but Bryson called during the afternoon and told me he may have to go to Dallas. I can't lie I got a little excited."

"Excited? You've only talked to him a couple of times. Am I missing something here?" Carrie asked.

Our waiter came over and asked if we'd like to start with a drink or appetizer.

"Yes I'd like a Vodka tonic with a lime," I told him.

"Pellegrino for me please," Carrie said.

The waiter couldn't leave fast enough.

"Pellegrino? Am I missing something here?" I asked Carrie.

"No. My stomach is a little upset that's all. But back to Brian."

"Bryson."

"Him."

"You're funny Carrie. Well, he's going to Dallas tomorrow and he asked me to come for the weekend."

"Did you tell him you're busy the rest of the year?" she asked.

I laughed.

"No I didn't."

"Why not?"

"I didn't tell him yes either. During the conversation I got annoyed thinking about how William used to ask me the same thing after we didn't get married."

"Exactly! You don't even know this guy. He could be a serial murderer working a great job."

"Carrie you're being extreme right now. He offered to buy my ticket and get me a separate room."

"It all sounds so inviting. But you're still busy the rest of the year." She laughed.

"I told him I could buy my own ticket."

"Are you thinking about going Sam?"

"I am actually. That's why I wanted to talk to you."

"Do you plan to sleep with him? I mean what are you expecting to come out of this visit?" she asked.

The waiter returned with our drinks and asked if we wanted to order an appetizer or were we ready to order our meals?

"Can we start with the crab artichoke dip please?" I told him.

"Sure. I'll put that in for you ladies," he said.

"No, I'm not going to sleep with him, Carrie. Are you crazy? I don't even-"

"You don't even what? Know him? That's my point, Sam."

"I know, but something feels right about him," I said.

"Didn't you tell me he just broke up with his girlfriend?"

"Yes but I'm not looking to marry him. It would be a little getaway to have some fun," I said.

"Well, I say go ahead then. You're single. But be careful Sam. He sounds vulnerable coming off a fresh break up," she said.

"I know. I haven't bought a ticket yet."

"Yeah, but you have the flight details memorized I'm sure," she said.

"No, I don't Carrie."

The waiter returned with the dip and told me a gentleman at the bar offered to buy me a drink. I couldn't see inside to see whom he was talking about. Carrie rudely told the waiter yes, she accepts the offer. The waiter said he'd be back shortly.

"Carrie you're hilarious."

"I don't see what the problem is," she said sipping her sparkling water.

"How's your stomach?" I asked.

"It feels a little better."

"Good, then you can have a drink with me," I told her.

"Not tonight girl. I don't want to force it. I have a meeting in the morning, and I need to be sharp," she said.

"Okay."

"So are you going to Dallas?" she asked.

"I don't know, the tickets are pretty expensive because it's last minute."

"Do you think it would be worth it?" she asked.

"He really seems like a nice guy."

"That wasn't the question Sam."

"Yes, I do."

"Well go and have fun."

We both laughed as the waiter brought me the drink from a stranger. He asked if we were ready to order.

"I'll have salmon with asparagus," Carrie said.

"May I have the crab cakes with steamed broccoli?" I asked.

"Thank you, ladies," the waiter said.

"When are you leaving?" Carrie asked as she smiled at me.

I just shook my head.

"I haven't bought the ticket yet silly."

"Yes but you know when you're leaving."

"If I go, Friday afternoon and coming back Sunday."

"Do you want me to check on Max for you?"

"Would you?"

"Of course because I know you're not telling your parents about this trip," she said smiling.

"You know me so well."

"Yes I do."

Carrie was the reasoning I needed to boost my confidence. It's not that I wasn't mentally capable of making a decision but she would tell me straight after her round of questioning. I hadn't ever done anything like this before. Carrie knew of a one-night stand I'd had with a guy I knew from college right after I broke up with William. I had unprotected sex with him and I was petrified for months that I had caught something. Luckily, I hadn't.

We enjoyed the rest of the evening laughing as we people-watched and ate our dinner. The waiter returned to check on us and told me another gentleman offered to buy me a drink but I declined. Two vodka tonics was my limit.

"Sam, if this thing doesn't work out with Brian, I'm telling you there's a lot of nice men to choose from right here in DC."

"His name is Bryson. What thing are you talking about?" I asked.

"You know what thing."

We finished our dinner and surprisingly Carrie ordered dessert. I couldn't remember the last time I saw her eat dessert. The crème brulee came and the waiter left two spoons. I couldn't help myself. I had to ask, "I thought your stomach was still upset?"

"It is but I saw someone order this and I had to have it. Please have some with me," she said.

We finished the crème brulee and I thanked Carrie for meeting me and asked her to apologize to Jonathan for me. She hugged me and told me that wasn't necessary and to let her know what day I was leaving for Dallas. She was so certain. I headed home thinking about the what-ifs about me going to Dallas. My conversation with my father played over in my head as well. My phone beeped. It was a text from

William telling me he saw the news about the hack, and he asked how my day was. I deleted his message and didn't reply.

Chapter 13

When I got home, Max was lying in his favorite spot enjoying the evening view of the city. He came over to me when I walked into the kitchen.

"How was your day?" I asked.

"Did you see anything fun down below?"

"Did you miss me?"

His eyes communicated with me the best they could as a response.

"Do you think I should go to Dallas and see Bryson?"

I stood and washed my hands. Max stayed in his spot and looked up at me as he stuck his tongue out. I gave him some food and fresh water then headed to my bedroom. I sat down on my bed and looked at the clock. It was a few minutes after 2 AM in Germany. I wondered if Bryson was getting ready to leave for the airport. How far was he from the airport? I stood up and went to my bathroom to take a shower. I turned on the water and stood there looking in the mirror as the water warmed. I thought about my life and how empty and routine it was. Carrie and Jonathan seemed as though they were heading into the M category soon. Although I told myself I was over William, maybe I wasn't because I hadn't really given anyone else a chance to get to know me.

Subconsciously I compared everyone to him not affording them a fair chance. Physically, I had been on many dates, but mentally I was calculating all the things each man didn't have. The truth of the matter was I didn't need them to be like William because those things are what kept me with him longer than I should have. I needed something I'd never felt before. The mirror started to fog from the steam of the showers. I wiped a small area to see my face. At that moment, I made a decision I hoped I wouldn't regret. I stepped into the shower, and the hot water immediately felt good and relaxing. I smiled thinking about my decision.

When I got out of the shower, I put on a pair of shorts and one of my dad's old t-shirts. I saw one of William's old shirts in the drawer. I pulled it out and went through the rest of my drawers to remove any other clothing of his. His clothes still being here would only continue to remind me of something about him and some memory attached to some event. I hadn't stopped wearing his athletic shorts or his undershirts. When I finished going through all of my drawers, I had a full trash bag of his old clothes. I took the bag to the kitchen to take out with the trash in the morning. I grabbed my laptop and sat on my bed. I turned the television on and opened up the Internet to begin searching for my ticket to Dallas. The fares hadn't changed since I checked earlier. As I searched the various travel sites, I found myself smiling. Max walked in and jumped onto the bed.

"Max I'm going to Dallas!"

He didn't seem excited like I was as he nestled next to me. I selected a mid-morning departing flight to Dallas and a late afternoon returning flight back home. When the screen got to the billing information, I didn't quickly input my credit card information. I sat there biting my bottom lip. I looked over at the dresser drawers that no longer had any of William's belongings then back to my laptop screen. The time remaining to purchase the ticket I had chosen was down 3:12. I jumped out of bed and ran into the kitchen to get my purse. I rushed back to my laptop to see the time remaining was less than 3 minutes. I pulled my credit card out and started inputting the sixteen digit number and three-digit code on the back. I still needed to input my billing address and the clock in the right corner was ticking down to 2 minutes. I heard my phone beep. I looked towards the kitchen then back at my laptop. I hadn't chosen my seats either. I continued inputting my billing information to complete my transaction. I hit the submit button and tossed my laptop on my bed to get my cell phone. I picked up my phone and saw it was an email from Bryson.

Hi Sam,

You're probably asleep, but I wanted to let you know I was at the airport waiting to board my flight. I hope I wasn't too forward asking you to come to Dallas. I will talk to you when I arrive in Dallas.

Until then,
Bryson.

I stood at my kitchen counter and read his short message two more times. I smiled and walked over to Max's favorite place and looked at the airplanes one by one landing at Reagan. I went to the B's on my contacts list on my cell phone. When I got to Bryson, I pressed the green *phone button.*

We're sorry your call cannot be completed. If you wish to make an international call, please contact customer service to discuss international calling plans.

Before I met Bryson, I didn't have a reason to have international calling on my cell phone plan. I looked at the clock on the microwave.

It was close to 6 AM in Germany. I dialed the customer service number of my cell phone carrier.

"Thank you for calling Sprint my name is Courtney how may I help you?"

"Yes, Courtney I need to add international calling to my plan," I said quickly.

"Okay, ma'am. Let's take a look at your account," she said.

I looked at the microwave and bit my bottom lip. I wanted to tell Bryson I bought my ticket before he took off. Courtney came back on the line.

"Okay Ms. Hunt I see you are receiving the Federal Government discount, you have unlimited data and minutes, and you're due for an upgrade. May I interest you in getting your upgrade this evening?" she asked.

"No thank you, just the international calling plan please."

"We have a couple of choices. Do you travel a lot?" she asked.

"No, I don't," I said rudely.

"Do you call a particular country often?" she asked.

I looked at the clock on the microwave again. I thought this would be a simple phone call. I was fidgeting with the napkin holder and rearranging the napkins.

"Can I have a plan for Germany please?"

"Yes, ma'am I can set that up for you."

"Thank you."

"My pleasure. Can I do anything else for you this evening?"

"No thank you." I hung up.

I had to enter Bryson's number with the international code first manually. The phone rang funny as I stood there with a stack of napkins in front me. The international number had rung four times. Maybe I had missed him. I turned from the beautiful stack of napkins and walked over to my couch preparing to leave Bryson a message. Would it be the first message he heard when he landed?

"Hello!" he said.

I exhaled and smiled.

"Hi Bryson!" I said excitedly.

"Hi there. I thought you'd be asleep. How are you?" he asked.

I was holding my cell phone with both hands like a high school girl sneaking to make a phone call on my parent's phone late at night.

"I'm well. Thanks for asking. Have you boarded your flight?" I asked.

"We're starting now."

"Bryson!"

"Yes, Sam!"

The tone of his voice gave me goosebumps, and I slowly walked over to my window. The last few flights were landing in the Nation's Capital.

"I bought my ticket to come to Dallas," I said shyly.

He didn't say anything right away. I heard the announcement of his flight boarding in the background.

"That's great Sam. Thank you," he said.

I could sense he was smiling. I hope he was smiling.

"Thank you for inviting me," I said.

"I'm glad you decided to come Sam."

"I am too. I'm looking forward to seeing you."

"We'll have a great time, and I meant what I said about getting you a separate room," he said.

"Bryson you don't have to do that."

"Are you sure? It's no problem really."

"Yes, I'm sure."

I heard the announcement for group 1 to board.

"What group are you in?" I asked.

"Group 1."

"I'll let you go so you can board."

"This isn't Southwest. I'll still have an aisle seat," he said laughing.

"Okay. I just thought you'd want to get onboard and get settled."

"That isn't more important than talking to you Sam," he said.

His voice was commanding and what he just said felt genuine.

"What do you want to do in Dallas?" he asked.

"Do you like museums?" I asked.

"Yes, I love them."

"We can do that and grab some food," I said.

"Okay, that's Saturday. What time do you leave Sunday?" he asked.

I heard the announcement for Group 3 to board.

"Are you going to board?" I asked.

"You're funny Sam. I'll board now," he said.

"Okay. Call or email me when you land in Dallas," I said.

"Don't hang up Sam."

His voice rendered me helpless again with his sexy tone. I was still holding my cell phone with both hands and smiling. I leaned against my window and pictured how he might be looking as he boarded his flight. I heard the flight attendant tell Bryson he'd have to check his bag to his final destination. My smile turned upside down.

"I'm sorry Bryson."

"For what?" he asked.

"You stood in the boarding area talking to me instead of boarding earlier," I said.

"A personal choice of mine," he said.

He was so calm about it. I looked at the trash bag of William's belongings and thought how this situation would have been a complete disaster if this had been him on the other end. I frowned at the bag and turned back to the window.

"What are you wearing?" I asked.

"Sweats, t-shirt, sweat jacket, and tennis shoes."

"No suit?" I asked.

"The flight's too long, and I don't have to go right in. So I'm casual this morning," he said.

"That's good. Well, I better let you go," I told him.

"Sam!"

"Yes!"

"I'm really excited to see you."

"I'm looking forward to seeing you too."

"Until then," he said.

"Safe travels handsome."

"Good night Sam!"

I hung up with Bryson and still had my cell phone in between both of my hands. I pressed it against my chest and smiled. It was close to 11 PM and past my bedtime. I put the napkins I had arranged so pretty back in the holder and I walked to my bedroom. I went into the bathroom to floss and brush my teeth. Max was already at the foot of my bed. It was as if he knew I'd be leaving because he rarely slept in my room. I crawled into bed and said a prayer for my future and my upcoming trip. Before I turned my night lamp off, I sent Carrie a text.

I bought my ticket. I'm leaving Friday morning, and I'm coming back Sunday evening.

Have fun!

Chapter 14

3:53 AM and I was wide-awake and didn't sleep my best. I sat up in my bed and turned on my night lamp. I looked at my cell phone, and the email with my confirmation number was the only email I had received. It was too early to go for a run outside, so I put on some workout gear and went to the small gym in my building. I was the first one in there, so I had to turn the lights and television on. I stepped onto the elliptical machine and plugged in my earbuds to listen to FOX news. Listening to all of the craziness going on in the world I had done 60 minutes on the elliptical machine before I realized it. I grabbed two sanitizer wipes to wipe down the equipment then I went over to the mats and did some core exercises before returning to my condo. I showered, got dressed, and made a cup of green tea. It was close to 6 AM, and I knew my dad was awake. I wanted to tell him I was taking his advice and about my trip. I knew he'd tell my mom in a subtle way so she wouldn't worry about me too much and call me every hour. My dad answered on the second ring.

"Good morning Sam."
"Hi, dad. Why do you still get up so early?" I asked.
"I wake up to the sun not an alarm clock baby girl."
Ever since I could remember, my dad never used an alarm clock.
"Dad guess what?"
"Oh lord. What?" He laughed.
"I'm taking your advice."

"What's his name?"

"Bryson Garrison and I'm going to meet him in Dallas."

"I'm glad to hear this Sam. Life's too short," he said.

"I know dad."

"Be safe. When are you going?" he asked.

"This weekend!"

"Oh, that's really soon," he said.

"Yes I know, but I think it will be fun."

"Do you want us to check on Max while you're gone?"

"No, Carrie's going to come by. Thank you though."

"How's she doing these days?" he asked.

"She's good. We met for dinner last night."

"Is she still with the same guy? I can't remember his name."

"Yes, she's still with Jonathan."

"That's nice. Well, I need to go for my daily walk. Will we talk to you before you leave?" he asked.

"Of course you will dad."

"I love you, Sam."

"I love you too dad. Tell mom I said hello and I love her."

"I will let sleeping beauty know." He laughed.

I felt relieved telling my dad about my trip. Being an only child, I've learned you're never too old to let your parents know when you're traveling. It's just me, so they need to know my last whereabouts in case something happens. They do the same when they travel. I changed Max's litter box and put a can of food in his bowl and some fresh water before heading into the office.

Carrie called me on my way to work.

"I thought you weren't going?" she laughed.

"I never said that."

"Well, you deserve to have some fun."

"I hope to. How are you this morning?" I asked.

"I'm tired this morning."

"Late night with Jonathan?" I asked.

"Not at all. I'm just tired," she said.

"Do you have a busy day?" I asked.

"I have a couple of meetings," she said.

"Any new clients?" I asked.

"One potential. That's one of the meetings," she said.

"Well, good luck. I'm pulling up to the office-parking garage. I'll talk to you soon," I said.

"We need to go shopping before you leave," she said.

"For what?" I asked.

"You need some new outfits for your trip, Sam." She laughed.

"I don't know Carrie. I'll let you know," I said.

"Well, you should at least get your nails done."

I looked at my nails. I hadn't had a manicure or pedicure in a while.

"We'll see Carrie."

"Okay! Let me know."

"I will do that."

"Have a good day Sam."

"You as well Carrie."

The office was somewhat back to normal after the Dallas hack. I needed to finish a few tasks before Friday. When I walked by the security desk, they spoke and smiled at me. I returned the greeting and smiled as I got on the elevator. When I got off of the elevator, I checked my cell phone to see how many hours Bryson had left in the air. He should be landing in three hours. I smiled and kept walking to my office. I logged into my computer and began reading and replying to emails occasionally looking at the computer clock in the corner.

Bryson should have landed by now, but I hadn't heard from him. The morning seemed to fly by, and it was after 12 PM. I sent Carrie a text message and told her we could get our nails done Thursday after work. She replied quickly with too many smiley face emojis. I loved that girl, but I was growing concerned. Last night at dinner hearing her not order a drink caught me totally by surprise.

Not hearing from Bryson was starting to worry me slightly but I couldn't pull myself to call or text him. I didn't want to appear overly concerned. I opened an Internet browser and checked the forecast in Dallas for the weekend. The weather was going to be in the 70s with a 20% chance of rain on Saturday and Sunday. I started thinking about what I was going to pack and how many outfits I was going to take. I didn't want to overpack nor check my bag. My office phone rang and interrupted my design thoughts.

"Hello, handsome."

"Hi, Samantha."

"How was your flight?"

"Not too bad. We hit some turbulence midway through the flight."

"Did you get some sleep?"

"No. I wanted to stay up to get ahead of the jet lag."

"Oh okay. I thought maybe your flight didn't take off on time since I hadn't heard from you."

I tried to be subtle with my concern.

"What time is it?" he asked.

I looked at the clock on my computer.

"1:16 PM. Why?" I asked.

"Remember what I told you about your birthday?" he asked.

I could tell he was smiling. I bit my bottom lip and smiled as well.

"That's sweet Bryson."

"I want that to be our little special thing if you don't mind."

"No, I don't mind. I was a little worried though," I said.

"I appreciate you. I didn't want to call too many times in one day."

"You can call anytime," I said.

I couldn't believe I said that so easily.

"What time do you arrive on Friday?"

"My flight gets in at 2:20 PM. I'm on American Airlines."

"Is it a direct flight?"

"Yes. I'll email you my itinerary."

"Thank you. Are you nervous?"

"Not at all, should I be?"

"No, but I realize we've only seen each other briefly at the conference and talked a handful of times."

"I'm a big girl Bryson."

I wasn't being totally honest with him. I was nervous as hell but trusting my instincts to go and hang out with him with no expectations. After all, he is just coming out of a relationship.

"Sam!"

"Yes, Bryson."

"It's still a few days away. I'll understand if you change your mind about coming."

His charm was so intoxicating. I felt my heartbeat increase as I bit my bottom lip and played with the telephone cord.

"I'll see you Friday," I said.

"Until then."

"How are things there in the office?"

"A little chaotic but I believe they've pinpointed where the breach came from?"

"China or Russia?"

"North Korea actually."

"Isn't that where that crazy guy is?"

"Yes, it is."

"Oh boy. That's scary."

"Did they get a lot of information?"

"They were able to get a few hundred thousand social security numbers and some folks' bank account information."

"I hope everything works out. Will you have to stay longer than you thought initially?"

"I shouldn't have to. Why?"

"I was just asking. I'm sure you have a lot going on in Germany."

"I do but my team there is really good. I couldn't ask for a better one."

"That's great."

"Sam, I don't mean to be rude, but I need to get back to the task here. Can we talk later?"

"Of course, talk to you soon Bryson."

"Until then."

"Thanks for calling handsome."

"Sam!"

"Yes!"

"I'm excited and happy you decided to come."

I was biting my bottom lip again, and the telephone cord was twisted up so tight that it looked like a long braid.

"I am too Bryson."

When we disconnected, I still had the telephone receiver in my hand as I stared off into space remembering Bryson's face and his masculine voice.

Chapter 15

The rest of the week flew by. I talked to Bryson a couple of times throughout the week. Carrie and I met to get our nails done at our favorite shop in Georgetown. They served wine, water, and tea. I ordered a glass of Chardonnay and passed the menu to Carrie. She told the young Asian lady she'd have a cup of green tea.

"Okay girl, what's going on?" I asked.

She leaned back on her chair and selected the massage settings before answering me.

"Nothing! Why?" she asked.

"The other night you didn't have a drink, and tonight you ordered green tea. Is there something you want to tell me?"

"No. I'm just not in the mood for alcohol. I'm good," she said.

I looked at Carrie as she started browsing through one of the current issue tabloids. I'm no mind reader but I was trying to see if I could pick up on any clues but Carrie's body language was silent. I picked up a tabloid and sat back as the Asian lady returned with our drinks. Carrie must have noticed my staring eyes because as soon as my chair leaned back, the interrogation started.

"How long will you be gone, Sam?"

"Just the weekend."

"A lot can happen in a weekend."

"True! But we're just going to hang out. No expectations."

"You don't have to convince me, Sam."

"I'm not trying to." I laughed.

Two ladies returned to our chairs and started our pedicures.

"So what do you guys have planned?" Carrie asked.

"We haven't talked about it."

"Are you going to before you get there?"

"I don't know. I'm really just going with the flow."

"Oh okay. Well, Dallas is a nice city."

"Yes. I'm sure there's enough to do, and it's only the weekend."

"I need a getaway myself," she said.

"Really? That came out of nowhere. Are you sure you're okay?"

"Yes I'm sure, but I could use some nice beach weather."

"Let's go somewhere in a couple of months," I suggested.

A puzzled look appeared on Carrie's face after I said that.

"Sure!" she said.

I wanted to ask again if she was okay, but I left it alone and relaxed as my feet were being massaged. I thought about what Bryson and I would do over the weekend to keep the devil's workshop closed. The Asian lady asked me what color would I like my toes painted. I pulled a dark plum polish out of my purse and handed it to her. She smiled and in her best English dialect told me it was a nice color. I heard Carrie tell the lady doing her pedicure she wanted French. That was so Carrie. I laughed silently to myself and continued looking at things to do in Dallas. The Internet page I had opened displayed activity options for families, couples, kids, and top weekend picks. Technically we weren't a couple, so I clicked on the "top weekend picks" link. A jazz festival, the state fair, a farmer's market, the aquarium, and the zoo were at the top of the long list of things to do. My phone vibrated.

"Hi, handsome."

"How's your day going Sam?"

His voice sent chills through my body as I listened and held onto every syllable of the words he spoke.

"It's going well and yours?"

"I just finished up a meeting."

"How are things going? Will you have time for me?"

"We've concluded the investigation of how they were able to tap into the system. Now we're securing things."

"Oh, okay."

"Of course I'll have time for you. I was worried you might change your mind."

"No. I was actually looking at things to do when you called."

"Is that right?"

"Yes! There's so much to do."

"What if I already have plans for us?" he asked.

The way he asked that question sounded slightly arrogant but sexy at the same time. He was letting me know he was a planner.

"What do you have in mind?" I asked.

"Do you trust me, Sam?"

That was an awkward question given we barely knew each other, and I was going to Dallas for the weekend.

"I don't know you well enough to answer that."

"So that means yes until I give you a reason not to."

"I wouldn't say it means that."

"It's similar to innocent until proven guilty."

"Right?"

I laughed at his analogy.

"That's fine Bryson."

"What's fine?"

"That you may have something already planned."

"Are you sure?"

"Yes, I'm sure."

"You didn't say whether or not you trust me?"

He was becoming annoying now with the trust question. How could he possibly think I could give him an honest answer? Maybe this wasn't such a great idea.

"Bryson, let's hope that we have a good time together."

Bryson didn't respond right away, and the silence was choking both of us. I was prepared to hear him tell me not to worry about coming to Dallas. I know that wasn't fair to him, but that's what I was accustomed to when the men of my past didn't get their way. William was a mastermind at manipulating uncomfortable situations that arose between us, and I'd give in without a second thought. I felt my spine turning into PlayDoh as the silence continued between Bryson and me.

"Sam, sorry about that, someone was asking me a question."

"Did you hear my last comment?"

"Yes, I did. I'm sure we'll have fun. See you tomorrow. Let me get back to the reason I'm here," he said.

"Okay, Bryson. See you tomorrow."

I felt a little uneasy the way we ended our conversation. I wasn't sure if I believed someone really asked him a question or if he was lying because his feelings had been hurt. Men act hard but their emotions are delicate like fine china. I'm sure Carrie had a million questions in her mental cue just waiting to ask. I went back to the Internet browser I had opened to see what other activities we could do in Dallas. The Asian lady finished painting my toes and slid the disposable flip-flops on my feet. I got up and walked over to an open manicure station next to Carrie.

"Was that him?"

"Yes that was Bryson."

"Is he excited you're coming to Dallas?"

"I believe so. I'm starting to get nervous now?"

"Why?"

I pondered the thought of telling Carrie about our conversation, but quickly decided against it. She wasn't being truthful with me about something and that bothered me. She had been there for me when William left me to announce the embarrassing news to my family and friends. If something was bothering her, why didn't she feel she could talk to me about it?

"I'm sure the trip will be great. You know how I overthink things sometimes," I said.

"Yes I do Sam. Have fun," she said.

"I plan to," I said as I handed the same nail color polish to the nail tech.

Silence invaded our favorite nail shop as Carrie and I sat getting our manicures without any words between us.

When our nails dried, we hugged each other and said our goodbyes not like best friends but more like two people who met for the first time in a nail shop and had small talk while our polish dried. I drove home listening to the Sirius XM jazz station to clear my thoughts and get back in my happy place. Between Bryson's unexpected question and Carrie's mood swings, I wasn't sure of anything and just wanted to relax. I needed to pack but now I wasn't as excited as I initially was. I need a long hot shower and a glass of Malbec.

I turned into my condo garage and the security guard was so pleasant with his greeting that I forced myself to smile back at him. Max must have heard my key in the lock because he was walking towards me when I walked in. He walked his furry body around my legs and I could feel his head rub against my leg. I bent down and rubbed him and gave him kisses. I heard him purr as he nestled his head against me. Oh how I wish I had a man who loved me as much as

Max. A man who would meet me at the door and ask me how my day was, rub my shoulders and kiss me softly on my lips. Then grab my hand and walk me to our bathroom and sit with me on the side of the tub as hot water filled the tub. As the tub filled he'd light a candle or two, stand with me, undress me slowly and help me into the tub where he'd wash my body making direct eye contact and kissing me on my cheeks, then my forehead. I can remember only one time William did this and he was in such a rush to finish and get back to some sporting event on the television that it wasn't enjoyable at all. Of course when the event was over, he wanted to be affectionate. No thanks! I became angry with myself for letting him interrupt my thoughts.

I went to the cabinet and pulled down one of my stemless wine glasses. I poured myself a glass of Norton Reserve Malbec before heading to take my shower. I turned on the shower and went to my other bedroom to pull out my carry on suitcase. My suitcase had a baggage claim check on it from Turks & Caicos. The last trip William and I took before I ended our *engagement*. I quickly ripped the tag off and tossed it in the trash.

The steam from the hot shower felt so relaxing. I tried as best as I could to let the water wash away the feelings that had changed my mood.

I wanted to erase the question Bryson asked me. I wanted to pretend it never happened and I was still excited about seeing him. I hadn't heard from him again, which further made me think he was serious about his question. It made me wonder if he had insecurity issues. The way Carrie and I parted was extremely odd and uncomfortable but I was never the pushy type and clearly she's going through something. I have to trust that our friendship has mutual value and that eventually she'll tell me what's troubling her.

I stepped out of the shower and dried off. I applied shea butter all over my body and wrapped the towel around me then went back to the kitchen. I checked my cell phone but I had no missed calls and no new text messages. I picked up my glass and took a sip of my wine and stared out of Max's favorite window. The city lights of DC were so pretty at night. As I stared off into the night I silently asked myself if this trip was a good idea or was I moving too fast? Did I trust Bryson not to put me in a compromising position? This trip could turn bad real fast. He was a director and I was a subordinate. I'd certainly lose my job first. I took another sip of wine and grabbed my cell phone before heading to my bedroom.

I put on a pair of shorts and one of my dad's old t-shirts and unzipped my suitcase. A framed pictured of William and I slapped me in the face. I pulled the picture out and put it through my shredder. I kept the picture frame. Hell it was a nice frame. I went to my closet and tried to think of what I should bring to Dallas. I heard my cell phone vibrating, but I didn't hurry over to answer it. I pulled down three pairs of dark jeans and looked for tops I thought would be casual enough but sexy too. I picked out one pair of black pumps and a light jacket for the evening in case we were still outside. My phone stopped vibrating, and the caller left a voicemail. I didn't stop what I was doing to check and see who called. I put a pair of my favorite flip-flops inside my suitcase. I packed four matching sets of undergarments. I looked over my sleeping attire but what I had in my drawers wouldn't be appropriate for this trip, so I packed baggy sweats and t-shirts. My cell phone started vibrating again, but I needed to finish packing before I changed my mind about going. I packed two pairs of shorts and tops just in case it was warmer than the forecast. The unanswered caller left a voicemail. I didn't check it. I went into my bathroom and grabbed my travel sized toiletries and hair care products. I looked inside my suitcase to see if I was forgetting anything. I realized I hadn't laid anything out to wear on the plane. I picked out a pair of comfy sweats and a shirt to match and my sneakers.

I sat on the side of my bed and took a sip of wine before I checked the voicemail messages. The two missed were from Bryson and Carrie. Both had left voicemails. Carrie left a message apologizing for her crazy behavior in the nail salon and said we'd talk when I got back from my trip and to have fun. I knew something was wrong with her, but I owed her the choice to share when she was ready. Bryson said he'd had a long day, but he was looking forward to spending a fun weekend with me. His voice sounded like the Bryson I had been talking to *before* the awkward question intruded. His message told me to sleep well but not oversleep and that he was still waiting for my flight itinerary. I totally forgot to send it to him. Just hearing his voice on the voicemail made me blush and forget about the earlier conversation.

Carrie sent me a text while I was listening to Bryson's voicemail.

Hey Girl, call me before you take off in the morning. I'm really sorry about tonight. I hope you have fun in Dallas with Bernard. Love you.

She just refused to get his name right. I loved Carrie. I couldn't go to sleep without calling her. She answered before the second ring.

"Hi, Sam!"

She sounded happy.

"Hey, Carrie! I got your voicemail and text."
"I'm really sorry Sam."
Before I could speak, I heard her crying and sniffling.

"Oh my God Carrie. What's wrong?"

I could hear the television in the background, but her whimpering was slightly louder.

"Carrie!"

I heard her sniffle and break down even more. Her cries were loud, and I felt whatever pain she was feeling.

"Carrie! I'll cancel my trip. Please tell me what's wrong."

More silence between us but I could hear the television.

"Sam!"

"Yes, Carrie I'm here."

"I'm pregnant."

Now I was silent. A part of me thought she was initially, but I didn't want to believe it. Not Carrie. She was the last person I'd think would get pregnant. She had always said she didn't want children. But I wouldn't judge. I needed to be there for my best friend like she had been for me.

"It's going to be okay. Have you told Jonathan?"

I could still hear her crying heavily. She mustered up a low response.

"No!"

"When are you going to tell him?"

"I don't know. He's thinking about quitting his job and going back to school."

"Well, you need to tell him soon so he doesn't quit his job just yet."

"I don't want him to think I'm selfish."

I wanted to ask a parental question about protection and how did it happen but now wasn't the time.

"You need to tell him, Carrie."

"I know. I'm just really sorry I treated you the way I did."

"It's okay."

"I'll stop by every day and check on Max."

"Thank you, Carrie."

"I hope you have fun, Sam."

"I'm sure I will."

Her cries stopped, and I could hear the evening news in the background. She told me she'd be okay and would tell Jonathan sooner than later. I felt relieved now that I knew what was going on with Carrie. I told her I would call her when I landed tomorrow. I told her I loved her and would help her with anything she needed. She told me she loved me too and appreciated my support. We hung up much different than how we parted at the nail shop. It felt like the Carrie I was used to. I emailed my itinerary to Bryson, and he replied moments later thanking me and said he was looking forward to seeing me. I didn't reply back. I was tired and needed to get some sleep so I wouldn't oversleep and miss my flight. I turned my night lamp off and lay down. Carrie was still heavy on my mind. I laid in the dark trying to fall asleep but I felt tears building, and it wasn't long after before I felt them rolling down my cheek. I wiped my face and closed my eyes.

Chapter 16

I stood in line to board my flight and saw a couple standing off to the side. They were kissing and whispering to each other. I saw her walk away and head towards the gate as he stayed behind. As she got closer to the gate, the guy walked over and gave her another hug. Then he held her hand as she walked up to the gate agent. Just before scanning her boarding pass, they kissed one last time, and I heard them say I love you to one another. I missed every part of that scenario in my life. As I moved closer to scan my boarding pass, I thought about what I was about to do and wondered if it would become something or nothing at all. I told Carrie I was going with no expectations, but inside I felt different. I wanted the fairytale ending. When I got to the row of my seat, an older woman was sitting in the window seat. The middle seat wasn't occupied yet. I had the aisle seat. I put my suitcase into the overhead bin and sat down.

"Good morning," she said.

"Good morning Ma'am."

"Are you going home or visiting Dallas?"

"I'm going to visit a friend."

"That's nice. Do they live in Dallas?"

"No, he's there on business."

"Oh is he your boyfriend?"

She was an older lady and chatty. Normally I wouldn't have been so talkative, but she really meant no harm.

"No Ma'am. Just a friend."

"You don't have to call me Ma'am." She laughed.

"Okay."

"My name is Emma Boote."

"Nice to meet you. My name is Samantha."

"That's a pretty name. I live in Dallas now, but I'm originally from Louisiana."

"Thank you. Why were you in DC?"

"I was visiting a friend." She winked at me.

I smiled at the elderly lady sitting next to me as I fastened my seat belt. I sent Bryson a text letting him know I was on my flight and it was on time. He replied right away with emojis. I sent Carrie a text and asked how she was doing.

It was time to power down cell phones, and I hadn't heard back from Carrie so I left mine on a little longer hoping she'd text me back. I hid my cell phone underneath my right leg as the flight attendants did their walk through checking seatbelts and tray tables. When I thought the coast was clear, I pulled out my cell phone hoping I had a text message from her before we took off. We were second in line for takeoff and Carrie hadn't texted me back. I felt my new friend's eye looking at me as if I was breaking the law by keeping my cell phone on. I heard the pilot tell the flight attendants we're next for takeoff. I turned my cell phone off and didn't like the feeling I had. I will call her when I land.

I was hoping Ms. Boote would fall asleep shortly after takeoff. That didn't happen. After the flight attendants served the complimentary drinks and pretzels, she started chatting up a storm.

"So what are you going to do in Dallas?"

"I'm not sure. My friend says he has some plans for us."

"What kind of food do you like?"

"I can eat whatever. I'm not a picky eater."

"There's so many nice restaurants in and around Dallas?"

"Oh, okay."

"What do you like to do?"

"I enjoy museums and a good zoo."

"Our zoo is great, and we have some nice museums. They're not free like the Smithsonian in DC but worth a visit."

"I will see if I can make it to one."

She leaned in closer to me before whispering her next line of questions.

"Are you and your *friend* looking to do anything romantic?"

I smiled at Ms. Boote before answering.

"We're not on that level."

She leaned closer again.

"I know some nice cozy places as well."

My smile returned.

"Oh yeah?"

"Yes."

"I don't think I'll need those places. But thank you."

She leaned back over into her window seat and winked at me again.

The rest of the flight she was quiet, and I watched an independent film about two people who had lost contact over the years but saw each other in a foreign country doing humanitarian work. They instantly reconnected and fell in love. I guess the window seat passenger was watching my screen as well. She tapped me on my shoulder to get my attention.

"Isn't love a wonderful thing, Samantha?" she asked.

"Yes, it can be if you're with the right person."

Ms. Boote frowned and then smiled before she spoke again.

"Samantha love isn't a person my dear."

I smiled at the elderly lady of wisdom.

"I know it isn't, but it's a part of love."

"Love is what you make it. It sounds like you're looking for perfection."

I smiled again at my new found love expert.

"No one's perfect, but yes I am looking for certain things."

"Like what?"

"Kind, loyalty, honesty, intelligence, selflessness, family oriented, and outgoing."

"And are you all of those things Samantha? What are you bringing to the table?"

I couldn't believe I was 35,000 feet in the air amongst the clouds having this conversation with a complete stranger elderly or not. I wasn't sure I wanted to continue this useless banter. Love was nowhere near me, and I didn't see it in my immediate future.

"I'm ready for love when it's ready for me."

"My dear no one's ever ready for love. It's not something you prepare for."

"I disagree. If we had met two years ago, my response would have been different."

"Someone broke your heart?"

"Into the smallest pieces."

"Love does that. But love also puts all the pieces back together, stronger than before."

"We shall see."

"Trust me I know. When my first husband passed away, I swore I'd be a widow until I died."

"I'm sorry to hear about your loss."

"It's okay. We were together forty-two years."

"That's great."

I didn't want to ask, but I became curious about who she was visiting in D.C.

"I know what you're thinking," she said.

I smiled but didn't answer.

"When I met Stan I had no idea it would blossom into what it is today."

"I'm happy you've found someone, Ms. Boote."

"My dear you young folks don't know anything about love. You run at the first sign of trouble and on to the next lust disguised as love."

The captain of our flight came on the PA system and informed us that we were 200 miles away from Dallas and we'd start making our initial decent shortly so now would be a good time to use the lavatory before he turns the fasten seatbelt sign back on. This was my chance to break away from my counseling session on relationships. Hopefully, when I returned to my seat, the window passenger with wisdom will be closed. As I unbuckled my seatbelt to escape Ms. Boote, she tapped my shoulder once more.

"My dear, have you ever heard the term *arduous*?"

"I can't say that I have?"

"Look it up, and that will tell you what love is."

She smiled at me with wide eyes and then looked out of her window. I smiled at her and got out of my aisle seat as quickly as I could.

When I got to the back of the airplane, there were two people ahead of me waiting to use the lavatories. As I stood there, one of the flight attendants got my attention.

"Now you're ready for a soul quenching relationship," she said laughing.

"Oh my God. She was a sweet lady but my goodness."

"I can't believe you kept the conversation going. You're so brave."

"I didn't want to be disrespectful."

"Hell you don't know her and probably will never see her again."

We both laughed as a lavatory became available. When I came out, the same flight attendant asked me if I wanted a glass of wine on the house. I kindly accepted before returning to my counseling seat.

We started our descent into the Dallas Fort Worth area, and Ms. Boote remained silent. When the wheels hit the ground, I powered my cell phone on before a flight attendant announced that we could. Carrie had texted me back. She apologized for not responding before I took off and said she was in the bathroom dealing with morning sickness. She said she was going to tell Jonathan that evening. My mom had called and left a voicemail wishing me a safe trip and said to call her when I land.

When we arrived at our gate, I stood up to get my suitcase from the overhead bin. Ms. Boote asked if I wouldn't mind getting hers down. She told me it was the leopard print one. I pulled her's down and sat it on the seat I'd received 3 hours of relationship counseling in and remained standing. As the passengers started getting off the plane, I checked around my area before moving.

"It was really nice meeting you," I said.

"Likewise my dear and good luck," Ms. Boote said.

When I got off the jet bridge, Bryson was waiting for me by a charging station. He was wearing a dark blue suit tailored to his body with a white shirt and a light blue tie with a pocket square in his jacket pocket and a pair of brown wingtip shoes. He looked more attractive than I remembered. He smiled as I walked towards him. His walk had distinction, and his posture seemed picture perfect.

"Hi, there!" he said.

He extended his arms and gave me a gentle hug. I was still shocked to see him at the arrival gate.

"How were you able to come to the gate?" I asked.

"I put my keys, wallet, and belt in the tray and took my shoes off before walking through security like everybody else." He laughed.

"Okay, smarty pants."

Just then I saw Ms. Boote walking our way smiling. When she got closer, she said, "He's handsome" winked and kept walking.

"Who was that?" Bryson asked.

"A nice elderly lady I sat next to on the plane."

"Is this all of your luggage?" he asked.

"Yes, it is."

"Are you hungry? What would you like to do?"

"I thought you had plans already?"

"I do, but that's later on this evening."

"I need to stop by the ladies room and make two phone calls."

"Okay, I'll wait here."

I called my mother to let her know I arrived safely. She told me to enjoy myself and to be careful. I called Carrie, but she didn't answer. I left her a voicemail and asked her to call me back. Bryson took my carry-on luggage and pointed towards the baggage claim, ground transportation, and parking signs. I knew it was too soon for us to hold hands but as we walked and our fingers brushed against each other, I wondered what his grip felt like. I looked around the terminal as we walked and took in the many walks of life in the airport leaving, connecting or arriving. I looked at Bryson's walk and instantly saw his confidence. His cheekbone looked relaxed but rigid, and his skin was acne free and didn't appear oily. His lips looked nice, and his bottom lip was slightly larger than his top lip. His mustache was trimmed sharply around his lip line. We didn't talk to each other until we reached the elevator.

"Are you hungry Sam?" he asked.

He smiled and looked directly at me. I caught myself before I bit my bottom lip.

"Sure. What do you have in mind?"

"I'm not picky. Do you want to eat an early dinner or just pick up something to snack on?"

"It depends. You never told me what you had planned," I said and smiled.

He smiled again before answering me.

"I thought we could take in one of the museums before they close. Then grab dinner and head to a speakeasy for some spoken word."

He really did have things planned out, and I couldn't complain. Everything sounded great. William would have kept saying I'm fine with whatever instead of taking the lead I digress.

"That sounds great. Let's head to the museum. I'm okay right now."

"Okay. If you get hungry, just let me know, and we can grab something to eat."

"Okay. Thank you."

We exited the elevator to the parking level where Bryson parked. The lights of a lime green Nissan Versa blinked twice. He opened my door first before putting my luggage in. When I walked by to get inside the car, he was looking directly at me and smiling. His skin looked so smooth and his eyes were mind-blowing. When I sat down, he told me to buckle my seatbelt before closing the door. I watched him walk to the back of the car and when I saw him approach his side of the car, I leaned over and opened his door slightly.

"I didn't think women did that anymore?" he said smiling.

"My mom does it for my dad."

"That's nice."

"Which museum are we going to?"

"I thought we'd check out the American History museum. Is that okay?"

"Sure that's fine. Are you a history guy?

"I do believe you have to know where you've come from to know where you're going."

"I can respect that." "If you don't mind me asking, where are you from Bryson?"

"I don't mind at all. I'm from a small town name Ocala in Florida."

"Where in Florida is that?"

He must get asked that a lot because he laughed before answering.

"It's about an hour from Tampa."

"Do you visit often? Are your parents still there?"

"No."

"No what?"

"I don't visit often, and my parents no longer live there."

His tone was slightly edgy.

"Bryson I apologize. I was just asking since…. well you know."

"It's fine Sam." He tapped my hand softly and smiled at me.

"You sure?"

"Sure. Ask away," he said.

I looked at him before I continued my questions. He looked relaxed and didn't seem bothered at all. I looked out of the window and pondered whether I should continue. There wasn't much traffic on the road by the airport, and I could see the planes one by one coming in for landing. I thought about Carrie and wondered how she was doing, and if she had told Jonathan he was going to be a father.

"So Sam."

I broke my stare and looked at Bryson.
"Yes."
"I'm glad you came to visit."
I smiled.
"I'm glad I did too."
"I was serious when I said you could ask me anything. That's how you get to know a person right?"
"True. But people tell you what they want you to know. You know only the good stuff."
"Sometimes. But eventually, everything comes to the surface, right?"
"Yes. If you're around long enough."
He laughed.
"What were you going to ask me a few minutes ago?"
My hesitation ever present and if he was totally honest would I be judgmental?
"Do you have any siblings?"
"Yes,, I have two younger sisters."
"Are you guys close? Do they live in Ocala? Did I pronounce it right?"
"Yes, you did silly. No, they don't. My youngest sister is finishing her degree in political science at Pepperdine University, and my other sister works for Nike and lives in Wisconsin."
"Oh, okay."
"What about you Sam?"
"I don't have any siblings."
"How was that growing up an only child?"
I guess this is the official icebreaker.
"At times it was lonely."
"I bet."

"How many years apart are you and your sisters?"

"I'm 18 months apart from Brooke and 3 years older than Brittany."

"Which one of your parent's name started with a B?" I laughed. Maybe that was a little rude.

"Neither actually. I'm not sure why they named all of us with the same first letter."

"Where do your parents live now?"

"My mother died a couple of years ago, and I haven't seen my father since Brittany's second birthday."

"I'm sorry to hear that Bryson."

"During her 2nd birthday party, he said he was going to the store to get some ice cream and never came back."

"Are you serious?"

Maybe I should have surrendered to my hesitation and sat quietly.

"Yes. I remember sitting in the bay window in our living room waiting for him. I watched car after car go by. His black SUV never pulled into the driveway."

I stared at him, and he didn't show any emotion recounting an awful memory thanks to me. Great job Sam. Then he slowly turned, and his beautiful smile was in full bloom.

"Bryson, let's stop with the questions for now."

"I'm fine really. I felt so bad for my sister because she kept asking 'where's daddy?' My mother kept saying he'd return soon. She must have known he wasn't coming back."

"Why do you say that?"

"Because she didn't seem worried at all. She didn't attempt to call him or anything."

"Oh, I see. That must have been tough."

"It was, but my mother was strong and pushed through it."

"Did your mother have any family to help her?"

For the first time, he didn't answer right away. I saw his cheekbone tighten.

"Yes, my Aunt Gladys and Uncle Raymond."

"That was good, right?"

He nodded his head up and down, and I saw his cheekbone relax. We exited the interstate, and within a few blocks, we were at the American History Museum. I didn't mean to come off snobbish, but it was much smaller than the Smithsonian back home. The parking lot looked full though. When we parked, Bryson didn't come around and open my door. He came to the back of the car and stood there. The weather forecast was accurate, and the temperature was mild, but I brought my sweater because the temperature inside was probably cooler. When I got out of the car, Bryson looked at me with no smile, more of a blank stare as if he was having second thoughts. I forced myself to smile at him before I started walking.

"Are you okay?" he asked.

"Yes. Again I'm sorry Bryson."

"Oh stop that. You didn't expect us to sit silently did you?" His smile was back.

"No, I didn't."

"Or talk about work?"

"Oh gosh no."

"May I?" he positioned his hand to hold mine.

Without hesitation, I interlocked my fingers with his manly but soft hands. I felt I owed him that comfort after the disturbing feelings I stirred up. When we got to the ticket window, I offered to pay for the tickets still feeling horrible. Bryson ignored my offer and politely told the window attendant 2 adult tickets. He paid for the tickets but never gave me my ticket. He stuck his hand out again, and once more I interlocked my fingers with his. He led the way as we entered the museum.

"Sam do you have to use the ladies room?"

"No, I'm good. Thanks."

"I need to hit the men's room. I'll be right back."

"Okay. Be sure to wash your hands." I laughed.

"What if I don't get anything on them?"

"Ewwww!"

He laughed and disappeared into the restroom. When he came out, he walked towards me with his hands in the air.

"You are silly," I told him.

"Do you want to smell them?"

"No silly."

And like that, we seem to be back in a happy place. We walked through the museum viewing the historic exhibits. Occasionally unlocking fingers due to the volume of other patrons or to look at an exhibition. We had been inside the museum almost 45 minutes, and Bryson hadn't looked at his phone one time. William would have been on his phone the whole time bumping into people checking emails. His job consumed him, and I dealt with that too long. Bryson was looking at a Civil Rights exhibit and turned to ask me…

"Do you vote every election?"

This could be another disastrous conversation.

"Yes. Do you?"

"Indeed."

"Even the mid-term, local, and government."

"All of them," he said proudly.

"Good."

"I wish people understood the voting process more."

"What do you mean?" I asked.

"Most people think the Presidential election is the *only* important one. They're all important."

"Yes, I agree with you there."

We moved on to the military and transportation exhibits. Of all the times I'd been to the Smithsonian in Washington, I never really paid much attention to the military exhibits. As I walked through I was enlightened by all of the casualties. I had heard of all the conspiracies behind Vietnam, but it didn't really interest me. I didn't know anyone who ever went in the military. My father and grandfather were anti-military but supported the troops for the sacrifices they made. I made a mental note to visit the war museums one day in the future. I felt Bryson reach for my hand breaking me from my patriotic thoughts.

"Would you have done it, Sam?" he asked.

"Done what?"

"What Rosa Parks did?"

My father always said one of the best first date places was a museum. You learn a lot about a person. Do they have patience? Are they cultured? Are they educated? Their likes and dislikes. Bryson asked a thought-provoking question that had raised mixed answers over the years from researchers.

"I don't know to be honest."

"Why not? Don't you think she was courageous to do what she did during that period?"

"Yes but it's been said she didn't do it to take a stand but merely because she was tired."

"I have heard that. You don't think other colored people were tired before her but still made the walk to the back of the bus?"

"I suppose you're right. During that time, our people were very fearful."

"A lot of our people are still fearful," he said.

"We can agree there, but honestly there are so many issues today. How do you choose just one?"

"Sounds like an excuse." He smirked and smiled.

"Okay, Mister. If you were king for a day what would you change?"

"I've never liked that question because it's not realistic. A king needs more than a day."

We both laughed.

"No, seriously, what would you do Mr. Garrison?"

"I would start with education. Slavery did more mental damage than physical. Would you agree?"

I didn't expect to have this kind of conversation on this trip. But I was enjoying the stimulating banter. We didn't have to agree on everything.

"Education is important. But we are in an instant gratification society. No one wants to put in the work. YouTube and Google beat the chalkboard any day."

"Good point but what if past activists gave up so easily?"

"Bryson I hear what you're saying. I just feel our society is selfish and doesn't care anymore."

"Well, I'm not giving up. When I finish my assignment in Germany, I plan to be active wherever I work next."

"That's great. From the sounds of it, you'll be great."

We sat and started comparing museums we'd both been to, and before you knew it, we had been there three hours, and it was closing soon. Surprisingly, I wasn't tired, but I was getting hungry.

"Do you mind if we grab some food?"

"Of course not."

"What do you have a taste for?" I asked.

"I can eat anything. You pick," he said.

"Any good seafood restaurants here?"

"I'm sure we can find something."

We stood up and walked to the exit. Our hands didn't touch immediately. I wasn't sure if there was tension after our conversation. I could tell from his tone that he had strong feelings about history and progression. When we reached the exit, just before walking outside, Bryson reached for my hand and held it gently but firm enough to let me know there were no hard feelings. I pulled out my cell phone and did a Google search for seafood restaurants in Dallas. The first one that popped up with 4.8 stars was Trulucks Seafood, Steak and Crab.

"I found one with 4.8 stars," I said.

"Sounds good. What's the address?"

He opened the passenger side door for me.

"Sam I enjoyed our time at the museum."

"I had a great time as well."

He typed in the address of the restaurant into the rental car GPS, and we exited the museum parking lot to our next destination. I was surprised Carrie hadn't returned my call yet.

"Don't forget we have plans this evening," Bryson said.

"Okay. After dinner, I need to go to the hotel and change."

"Yes, so do I."

It didn't take us long to get to the restaurant. The atmosphere was casual but cozy. It had a live band playing, and there were only a few open tables. Bryson walked up to the hostess and told her table for two. I heard her ask if we had reservations and Bryson replied with a disappointing no. The young lady told him it would be an hour wait, but the bar was open seating. Bryson turned to me and asked if I minded sitting at the bar. I looked over at the bar area then back at Bryson with an approving nod. We found two openings at the bar.

"How much time do we have?" I asked.

Bryson looked at his watch.

"We are good on time," he said.

The menu was a seafood lover's dream. I spotted the scallops and creamed spinach on the menu. The bartender greeted us and took our drink order. I ordered a vodka and tonic. Bryson ordered a whiskey Manhattan. When our drinks arrived, Bryson lifted his glass. I took a sip of my drink first.

"To endless possibilities!" he said.

Chapter 17

Bryson ordered the miso-glazed sea bass with asparagus. We enjoyed the live entertainment and occasionally smiled at each other but didn't talk too much during dinner. When the band took an intermission, Bryson broke our silence.

"Sam, I hope you don't think I'm some race radical."

"Not at all. It's nothing wrong with having a strong passion for something."

"I apologize if I was obnoxious."

"Oh stop. I'm fine."

"Okay. Thank you."

"I'm ready if you are. I need to freshen up, remember."

He got the bartender's attention and asked for the bill.

"I can pay for my meal Bryson."

"I'm sure you can, but that isn't necessary."

"It's no problem."

"Sam, please allow me to be a gentleman."

"Thank you for the dinner Bryson."

"You're welcome."

Leaving the parking lot of the restaurant, I initiated the contact and rested my hand on top of his as he drove. He looked at me with those soul burning eyes then smiled just enough that I could see a small dimple for the first time.

We pulled up in front of a tucked away boutique hotel. The small sign read The Vagabond. A valet ran up to my side and opened my door and greeted me with a warm welcome. I stepped out of the car and took in the area. It looked like we were in an old town setting. There were restaurants, shops, and a couple of ice cream shops. The roads looked like old cobblestone.

"Is this okay?" Bryson asked.

Bryson was standing on the sidewalk with my carryon luggage waiting for me. I took one last look before walking towards him. I was looking for a street name or something to give me a landmark. My paranoia meter was to the far right at this moment.

"Come on Sam, it's okay."

Bryson must have caught my disturbed look. I walked cautiously towards him. When I got close enough, he reached for my hand. The small foyer didn't ease my uneasiness. The front desk clerk acknowledged Bryson as Mr. Garrison and me as Ms. Hunt. I smiled and spoke back. The elevator looked European in size. When Bryson pushed our floor, I couldn't help but ask.

"How did she know my name?"

"I told the hotel staff that I had a guest visiting."

"And you had to tell them my name?" I sounded annoyed.

"Are you bothered by that?" he asked.

I sulked a little bit and folded my arms. I wasn't used to this type of treatment. I was being bratty and unfair to Bryson. I couldn't help it. When I traveled with William, it was always about him, and I felt like the flavored pleasure of the trip.

"I apologize Bryson."

"No problem. I should have told you."

He's such a charmer with his sincerity. I smiled and leaned on him while the elevator climbed to our floor. The number on the door was

14, but we were on the fourth floor – the top floor. Bryson opened the door and said, "After you."

The room was Mediterranean looking in décor. The floors were stone, and the walls were painted a light bronze. There was a small kitchen off to the right with a single sink and an electric stove with two burners. The refrigerator was white, and the countertops looked like some type of quartz. The cabinets were dark brown and looked painted over. The living room was small with a small sofa and flat screen television. There were closed doors to the left and right of the living room.

"Sam, your room is on the right."

"My room?"

"Yes! I thought you'd want your own space being it's our first official 3-day date."

I looked at him as he stood there with my luggage. I can't believe a boring conference, and an international phone call had brought us to Dallas for our first date. To make it even better, he was the ultimate gentleman. I broke my stare to thank him for his thoughtfulness.

"Bryson you don't have to do that. Thank you."

"No problem. I'll set your luggage inside the room for you."

"Okay thank you."

"There are four sets of towels in there and a Turkish bathrobe if you'd like to wear it."

"Okay. I should be ready in 30 minutes."

"Take your time."

He walked to his bedroom and left the door open. I closed my door and sat down on the queen-sized bed. I pulled out my cell phone and called Carrie. She didn't answer. I pulled out a pair of the jeans and one of the tops I packed. I put the blouse on a hanger from the closet and put it on the back of the bathroom door for the steam to knock the wrinkles out. I turned on the water in the shower and started to undress. I thought about locking the bathroom door but decided against it. Something told me I could trust Bryson. When I saw the steam forming, I grabbed my body wash and jumped in the shower. I lathered my body and thought about Ms. Boote and smiled. I rinsed off and grabbed one of the oversized towels from the hanging rack. I wiped the mirror and tried to decide if I was going to wear makeup or not. I put some deodorant on, applied shea butter to my body and put on one of the matching bra and panty sets. I pulled out my makeup bag and pulled out my eyeliner and one of the lip pencils from the MAC store. The steam did the job I wanted it to. I got dressed, put on the wedge heel I packed, and I put my driver's license, some cash, a credit card, a lip pencil and a compact in a small purse I brought along. When I walked out into the living room area, Bryson was still in his room getting dressed I presumed.

"Bryson, I'm ready when you are."

"Okay! Give me a few minutes."

"No problem."

"Sorry about that," he said.

He came out in a pair of dark jeans fitting nice with a small checked long sleeved shirt with the cuffs turned back and a pair of brown loafers. I could smell his cologne. It was one of my dad's favorite – Issey Miyake. I stood up, and I don't know what made me do it, but I asked him to take a selfie with me. He smiled, and I felt his arm go around my waist. Then he quickly removed it and apologized.

"Sorry, it was for the picture."

"It's okay. You can put it back."

"You sure?"

"Yes, we are not teenagers silly."

His manly grip returned to my waist, and it felt good. We both smiled for the selfie.

"Are you going to send that to me?"

"Sure."

"Do you think I need a jacket or sweater?"

"Your call."

I went and grabbed the light jacket I'd packed.

"I'm ready."

When we got downstairs, the valet had Bryson's rental car waiting for us. I got in and didn't ask where we were going. I was going with the evening plans.

We pulled up in front of a dimly lit building with a line of people waiting to get in. The bright purple neon sign in front said *The Posh*.

"Are you ready?" Bryson asked.

"Let's do it."

The night air was a little chilly. I was glad I brought my jacket. Bryson came to my side of the car and took my hand, and we walked to a red rope ahead of the line of people waiting.

"Bryson, have you been here before?"

"No, I haven't. Why do you ask?"

"Just wondering how you got the VIP treatment."

"A little money helps." He winked.

We walked up a flight of stairs into a medium size room. The stage was small, and there was standing room only. Someone was on stage reciting a poem about pro-life.

"Would you like a drink?" Bryson whispered.

"Sure."

"Vodka tonic?"

"Yes. Good memory."

"Be right back."

"Bryson."

"Yes."

"No funny business okay."

"Of course not."

I watched him walk to the bar until I lost him in the crowd. I didn't think he would put anything in my drink, but you hear the stories of women waking up half dressed and violated. I listened to the lady on stage finish her poem.

"Vodka tonic for the lady."

"Thank you!"

Bryson held his cup up to mine.

"To endless possibilities."

"Salud."

We stood there amongst the other eager ears and minds waiting for the next artist to speak thought-provoking poetry. The next few poets talked about politics, good and bad sex, black lives matter and guns. While we stood there, Bryson whispered in my ear, "I'm glad you came Sam." I could feel his warm breath on my ear. When I turned to comment, our cheeks touched and we froze in that moment. In the dimly lit room where people exercised their freedom of speech, our eyes were locked on each other. I could see his striking glow, his dark eyes that were silently penetrating my soul. He had a slight smile on his face as he took a sip of his Whiskey Manhattan. I leaned in and kissed his full lips. He welcomed my intrusion and slid his tongue into my mouth. I felt myself exhale as I slowly let my tongue touch his. We became invisible in that poetic room. Bryson used his free hand and pulled me into his hard body. The way he kissed me was intense. It was perfect actually. No one had ever kissed me that way. I pulled away, and I could feel my heart racing. I took a sip of my drink. Bryson never took his eyes off of me, and his look was mesmerizing. I smiled at Bryson and stepped closer to him and slid my hand inside his shirt. His chest felt muscular. I saw him look down at my hand. He came in to kiss me again, but I put my fingers up to his lips. Then moved my hand to the side of his face and squeezed the back of his neck. I whispered in his ear.

"Let's get out of here."

He turned up his Whiskey Manhattan, then guided me to the flight of stairs to exit. I was surprised at myself, but the mood was amazingly romantic. I didn't feel any guilt. When we got outside, Bryson stood behind me with his hands around my waist. We kissed passionately while the valet got the car. His lips were so soft and I found myself pulling a little extra on his bottom lip. When we got in the car, Bryson held the steering wheel with one hand and mine with the other. We couldn't keep our eyes off of each other. When we came to a red light, he leaned over and kissed me. My heart was racing but the moment was intoxicating.

Inside the room, our kisses continued at the same intense speed. We squeezed each other. We pulled at each other's clothes. Then it was as if time stopped as Bryson slowly raised my blouse over my head. His touch was magical. I saw him look at my breasts and smiled. I started unbuttoning his shirt and felt his chiseled body. Bryson's chest was bare and muscular. I didn't see any ink spots. I felt him move me towards his bedroom and I didn't stop him. Inside his bedroom, he sat me down on the side of the bed and knelt down to take off my shoes. Then he came up to unbutton my jeans. His eyes were focused on me as he effortlessly undid my jeans and slid them down. I went to undo his pants and felt a bulge in his pants. I bit my bottom lip as I slid his pants down. He was a briefs man. Bryson slowly pushed me up further in the bed and laid slightly on top of me. Our lips met once more, and I felt his hands squeeze one of my breasts. I moaned softly and grabbed his thigh. He stopped kissing me and reached over to a small leather bag, and I saw him pull out some condoms. He saw my look of hesitation.

"Sam, we don't have to," he said.

I looked into his eyes, then at his chiseled cheekbones and a small dimple.

"No, it's fine Bryson."

I felt his hands at my hips sliding my panties down, and my body shivered a bit. A man hadn't touched me since William. Bryson's hands felt strong but soft. I sat up to take my bra off. His eyes explored every inch of my body as I did so. I tossed my bra on the bed and pulled down his briefs. His bulge was growing right before my eyes. I saw him look at me then he kissed me softly. He slid on the condom and eased on top of me.

"Sam, you look so beautiful."

I didn't know what to say, so I smiled. He kissed me again, then he kissed one of my breasts. I felt his right hand softly rubbing on my clit. I was already wet. He kissed me once more then I felt him ease inside of me. His bulge wasn't a figment of my imagination. His size filled me up, and I slid away slightly.

"Are you okay? I'm sorry," he said.

"Yes, it's been a while," I said.

"I'll be gentle."

"You are."

"You feel so good Sam," he said as he slowly slid in and out of me.

My eyes closed for a moment as the moans began to escape my mouth. Then I opened them quickly because his stroke was so electrifying I found myself thinking of William and I almost called his name. Bryson was so gentle yet erotic. I felt all of his muscular body against me with each stroke.

"Oh, my goodness Sam."

"Yes, Bryson."

"You feel so damn good."

"So do you."

We kissed some more then Bryson pulled me over on top of him. I slid down real slowly onto his rod of steel. He had me filled so well that my hips slowly grooved with him. He grabbed my breasts and played with my nipples. That turned me on and sent me to the moon. I stared down at Bryson as I rode him with my hands on his chest. He looked so sexy looking at me. I felt myself about to climax. My body started shaking a bit, and the speed of my ride increased as he slid a little deeper inside me. I leaned down to kiss him, and I felt his hands grab my ass. His grip wasn't too tight, but I felt his manly strength. He was close just like me. His hands started guiding my groove, and our heavy breaths joined in sync as we climaxed together. I let out a low scream and called Jesus name. I fell to the side of Bryson with my hands resting on his beating chest.

"That was incredible," I said.

"Yes, you were Sam," he said.

He kissed my cheek and slowly started rubbing my back.

Chapter 18

I woke up with Bryson's shirt on that he wore the night before. He wasn't in the bed, but I could hear him in the kitchen. I slowly got up and walked towards the kitchen. My body felt the workout from last night. Bryson saw me.

"Good morning," he said.

"Good morning."

"Coffee? Tea or Juice?" he asked.

"What kind of tea do you have?"

"Let's see… they have Lipton, Earl Grey, and an Orange spice here."

"I'll take the Lipton."

"Milk? Sugar or honey?"

"Honey please."

"Coming right up."

Bryson had on a pair of lounge pants with no shirt. Just looking at him I wanted to get my tea to go and head back to that magical place from last night.

"What time is it?" I asked.

"A little after 9 AM. How did you sleep?"

"Very well. What about you?"

"I slept great as well. Do you want some breakfast? I can order room service."

"Are you eating?" I asked.

"I normally have a protein shake. But please order what you like."

"No, the tea is fine."

"Sam, seriously order breakfast." He placed the menu in front of me.

"What's on the agenda today?" I asked.

"After breakfast, I was thinking we could visit a museum or two."

"That sounds good."

"See anything on the menu?" he asked.

"Bryson, I don't have to order breakfast."

"You sure? I'm ordering the buttermilk pancakes with sausage."

"So much for the protein shake," I said.

"One day of carbs won't kill me. Don't judge me," he laughed.

"I'll have the English muffin with fruit please."

"Done."

I sipped on my tea and listened to Bryson place our breakfast order. He was so kind and polite to the person. His smile even this early was so attractive. When he was done placing our order, he came over and sat next to me at the counter. He rested his hands on my thighs and squeezed them softly. Then he kissed me.

"Sam, do you mind if I take a shower before our food arrives?"

"Of course not."

"Thanks."

When he went to the bathroom, I grabbed my bag to check my phone. My parents and Carrie had texted me. I replied to my parents and told them I was doing well. Carrie's text simply said, 'I told him. We'll talk when you get back, and I hope you're having fun.' I replied with an emoji smiley face. I heard a tap at the door. I dug through my bag for a pair of my sweats to put on. When I opened the door, the hotel worker greeted me and asked where I would like the serving table set up. Just as he was uncovering the dishes, Bryson came out of the bedroom.

"Good morning, Sir, and thank you."

"You are most welcome. Please sign here."

"Have a great day," Bryson said.

"Sam, can I get you anything before I sit down?"

"No thank you."

He sat down and bowed his head. I heard him say Amen. Afterward, he reached for my hand and squeezed it softly before he started eating.

"When do you head back to Germany?" I asked.

"I leave Monday."

"Did you extend your stay because of me?"

His smile gave me my silent answer.

"Yes, I wanted to see you. I hope you don't mind?" he asked.

"That's flattering. You didn't have to do that."

"I didn't know when or if the opportunity would present itself again."

"I'm glad you did. I'm having a great time."

He smiled again, and I saw one of his dimples.

"Do you have a lot of work waiting for you in Germany? This was a last minute trip," I said.

"It's not too busy, and like I told you, I have a great support team."

"That makes a huge difference. Good for you," I said.

"What about you? Does the DC office keep you busy?" he asked.

"Yes! We just completed a major upgrade for all of the offices in DC, Maryland, and Virginia," I said.

"Oh, okay."

"We have to do the same for the west coast offices in the coming months," I said.

"I'm sure you'll get it done with ease. How is your team? Do you have a lot of contractors?"

"I have a decent mix of Government employees and contractors. How are the Germans in cyber? Any other nationalities working over there?" I asked.

"The Germans are truly efficient. Most of them were educated in the U.S. We have a few Russians on the team."

"Russians? Really?" I asked.

"I know that sounds a bit strange, but the relationship is exceptional."

"What clearances do they have?"

"Top Secret with poly," Bryson said.

"Wow! Most Americans don't have Top Secret with poly."

"True. They started working with the Government right out of college," he said.

"I guess a few bad parties won't put a blemish on your record," I said.

We both laughed. I was wondering if he would ask what level my clearance was or if he knew already. I didn't ask him his. I assumed being a director overseas, it was Top Secret with poly or higher. I finished up my breakfast and my now warm tea, and he finished his breakfast. Sitting here with him, I noticed he hadn't pulled out his cell phone one time to check it. That got him major points with me. Most times I was never William's main focus. I smiled as I watched him take the last few bites of his breakfast.

"Bryson, I'm going to take a shower so we can get this day started."

"Of course. I'll get dressed while you're in the shower. Would you like the morning paper?" he asked.

"No thanks. I won't take too long," I said.

"Is that even possible?" he asked and laughed.

"Funny man. See you in a bit."

"Take your time Sam, seriously. I was just joking."

I smiled at him before walking to the unslept in room. As I looked into my suitcase, I heard a knock at the door.

"Yes!" I said.

"You don't have to shower in there."

"I appreciate that, but I'll shower in here."

"Okay. Take your time," he said before walking away.

I walked into the bathroom and was surprised at the size. It had two large sinks, a Jacuzzi tub and glass enclosed shower with brown stoned walls. I turned on the shower and slid out of my sweatpants. I caught a glimpse of myself in the mirror still wearing Bryson's shirt from the night before. The top two buttons were open, and the cuffs weren't fastened. I grabbed one of the collars and smelt his cologne. The scent was still lingering and just as intoxicating as it was last night. I unbuttoned the shirt and took it off slowly letting it drop to the floor. I thought to myself, I wonder if he'd miss it if I took it back with me. I grabbed my loofah sponge and body wash and stepped into the hot shower. As the water splashed against my body, I had flashbacks of last night and immediately smiled. My body felt so relaxed as I began washing up. I thought about the way Bryson handled my body so passionately as if he had studied it before we kissed and had sex. Even though love was nowhere in the area, it felt like he made love to me instead of sex. His touch, his stroke, and the way he kissed me were mesmerizing.

I finished up in the shower and got dressed. I didn't bother putting on make-up. I applied some lip-gloss and used my eyelash brush. When I came out of the bedroom, Bryson was ready and looking at his cell phone. I walked up to him and kissed him on the forehead. He put his phone in his pocket, stood up and kissed me on my lips.

"Thank you for coming," he said.

"Thank you for inviting me."

"My pleasure. I hope I can see you again real soon," he said.

There it was, an invite to see me again. I wasn't sure how to respond, so I smiled. He quickly said, "No pressure Sam."

In less than 24 hours, he had thanked me for coming. The appreciation meant volumes he would never understand. He grabbed my hand and we headed out of the door to the museum. The weather was as the forecast stated.

We spent the rest of the day visiting two museums and eating at a diner off the beaten path. I had never heard of it and Bryson said he hadn't either. The food was very good. I ordered a Cobb salad and he ordered an open face turkey sandwich. I noticed he didn't eat the bread and not much of the stuffing. We continued to hold hands the whole time we were out and kissed in between conversation. We skipped dinner and snacked on two tuna packs from the hotel grab and go shop. That night we had sex multiple times and explored more positions than the previous night. Our energy levels were in overload because we stayed up all night talking to each other. It was as if we didn't want Sunday to come. We tried to outlast time.

"So what happened with you and your ex?" I asked.

"To be honest, I really don't know."

"Why is that?"

"I was honest with her about my job and she said she could handle it. But in the end, she couldn't."

"Did you guys try and compromise at all."

"I felt like she was starting to take me for granted."

"How so?"

"I felt like I was doing all of the calling and visiting."

"How often did you guys talk and see each other?"

"We talked every day and tried to see each other every three months."

"What happened?"

"She started texting more than calling and the excuses why she couldn't come increased."

"Do you think she was cheating?"

"The thought crossed my mind but she wasn't."

I didn't want to sound offensive.

"How do you know for sure?"

"What field do we work in?" He smiled.

"Touché. Do you miss her?"

"I used to."

"Do you feel like you're over her?"

"Yes."

"Are you guys still friends?"

"I haven't talked to her in months, so I really don't know?"

"No German girlfriend?"

"No. They're great people but after Stephanie I buried myself in work."

He said her name for the first time in the conversation. I wasn't going to ask her name.

"I know how that is," I said.

"What about you and William?"

I didn't answer right away although I knew the answer.

"It's okay Sam. We just met and I shouldn't have asked."

He was so freaking charming and considerate. I grabbed the side of his face and smiled.

"I'm over him. He calls when he's in DC hoping I'll come to his room."

"Oh, I see."

I could see on his face he wanted to know how many times I had given in.

"I won't lie Bryson. I used to do that when we first broke up."

"How long has it been?"

"Almost two years now."

I could see his mental calculator trying to come up with how many times had I given in. I touched his hands hoping he would sum up a small number of visits or let the thought fade away. I didn't want to answer truthfully because that would more than likely damage the good vibe and I wouldn't feel good about myself. Bryson was a great listener. Not once did he bash William. He even asked me if I still loved him. I paused before answering that question. A solid no should have been easy to roll off of my tongue, but the truth was I did still love him. My pause gave my answer.

"It's okay Sam. That's life. He's a lucky man."

"No he's not."

"Sure he is. To have a woman like you still love him is remarkable."

His damn charm was sickening.

"Do you still love Stephanie?"

It was childish, I know.

"No, I don't."

"How can you be so sure?"

"Because I gave my all and it wasn't enough. It's hard to still love someone after that."

His statement was profound but simplistic. It hit me like a category 4 hurricane. He continued.

"I did everything I could think of to keep the fire blazing not just burning," he said.

"I know what you mean."

"Do you?"

His voice was intense now and I could tell the good but mostly the bad memories were coming alive again.

"I sent roses."

"I called multiple times a day."

"I sent things just because not just on holidays."

"I bought last minute airline tickets when she said she had to see me."

"I sent her poetry."

He talked nonstop of his countless efforts to show his love and admiration only to be disappointed in the end.

"I'm so sorry Bryson. It's her loss."

His smile was gone, and his face was tight now. I could feel his pain. I saw him look out of the window of the hotel bedroom as the sun was rising. He stared in silence for a few moments.

"Sam, I'm truly sorry for blowing up like that. This was supposed to be our time."

"No apology needed. I've enjoyed every minute of it. It's how you get to know a person."

"You're not upset?" he asked.

"Of course not, silly."

He slid down on the bed and asked if he could lie in my lap. I told him of course.

I sat there with Bryson resting his head on my leg watching the sun come awake across the East Texas skies. I gently rubbed the side of Bryson's face and he rested his hand on top of mine in silence. Our heart to heart conversation overshadowed the earlier uninhibited sexual activity and made the beginning of our friendship bond strong. We entrusted one another with the deep lurking painful scars of love that we had endured.

Chapter 19

The rest of the morning was spent laughing and talking about how much fun we had the last couple of days. We talked about some of the people-watching we did while we were out and the wonderful exhibits we saw at the museums. I repacked my suitcase including Bryson's shirt. I never spent a night in the room he paid extra for.

"Do you have everything?" he asked.

"Yes, I believe so."

"If I find anything I can always mail it to you."

"Thanks but I'm sure I have everything."

"Okay. I'm certainly not rushing you but I don't want you to miss your flight," he said.

"Me either. Although I could stay another day with you."

"Next time."

He kissed me before he left the room.

Bryson held my hand the entire ride to the airport. He didn't pull up to the departure curb to let me out. Instead, he parked in short term parking and walked with me to security.

"Sam, don't go through security yet," He said.

"Sure. Is something wrong?"

"Not at all. I'm just not ready to see you go. I want to see you again. Is that possible?"

I thought about the couple I saw before departing Washington.

"I would like that Bryson. I don't want to rush anything though."

"I understand, and we don't have to. I enjoyed your company, and that's not the sex talking."

I giggled out loud. I wasn't ashamed. The sex was amazing.

"I enjoyed my time with you as well Bryson, and I'll say it for both of us. The sex was great." I laughed.

He smiled, and his dimples were back.

"And about earlier this morning," he said.

I placed my fingers over his lips. I felt him push his lips out kissing my hand. I shook my head.

"Everything was great Bryson."

I moved my hand from his lips and kissed him. People were walking around us to enter the security line. I felt like nothing or no one was around us, and we were in a small capsule surviving on each other's breaths.

"I hope to see you again soon Sam, seriously."

"Me too Bryson."

We kissed once more before I entered the security line to board my flight. I looked back occasionally, and Bryson was still there watching me make my way through security. When I put my suitcase on the x-ray belt, I looked and saw him wave and blow me a kiss. I returned the wave and kiss. I bit my bottom lip before I turned and walked through security. I grabbed my things from the x-ray belt and looked back to see if I could see Bryson, but he was gone. I exhaled, then headed to my gate.

When I got to the gate, my flight was pre-boarding its elite club members and passengers with small children. I heard my phone ringing. I pulled my cell phone from my purse. The caller ID displayed B. Garrison.

"Hi."

"Hi, beautiful. Are you at your gate safely?" Bryson asked.

"I am."

"Great. Is it too soon to tell you I miss you?"

"No, not if it's the truth."

"Sam, I truly miss you. I wish the sun could have stayed asleep a few more hours."

"I know I enjoyed myself. I can't remember the last time I stayed up all night doing anything."

"Me either. You're special Sam."

"Thank you, Bryson."

I heard the gate agent call my group number to board.

"Are you boarding yet?" Bryson asked.

"Yes, they just called my group. I will call you when I get to my seat."

"Until then."

I already loved how he said until then. It made me feel important to somebody. It was just goodbye or talk to you later. It was an incomplete sentiment waiting for the other party to complete it. It meant the other party was waiting to hear back from you and you weren't an afterthought.

When I got to my seat, I called Bryson back. He answered excitedly and said, "That took too long." He laughed.

"You're cute."

"Can you call me when you land? Do you need a moment to yourself?

"Sure, I can do that."

"Stephanie never called until she was off the parking shuttle and in her car in traffic. By then, she'd be upset with traffic and our conversation would be very short."

I didn't want to stay on memory lane too long.

"Oh no, I'll call you as soon as the wheels touch the ground. I'm sorry you didn't feel appreciated Bryson."

"It's fine. I shouldn't have brought her up. It's just she's the last woman I've seen take off from an airport."

He really did love her and gave his all. I could tell.

"I understand. Call you when I land."

"Until then."

"Drive safely back to the hotel."

"Will do. I miss you, Sam."

"Miss you too B."

"Is that my name now?"

I can't believe I called him that. I laughed. "Do you mind?"

"No. I've been called worse." He laughed.

"Talk to you soon handsome."

"I like that. No one's ever called me that."

"Doors are closing. I have to turn my phone off now."

"Miss you." I heard him blow me a kiss.

I did the same and powered down my phone just as the flight attendant made it to my row.

My flight home was less conversational than my flight to a weekend nothing shy of perfect. When I landed, I called Bryson. His response was romantically stimulating.

"I miss you already."

I looked around the economy seating to see if anyone was looking at me. I felt myself blushing as I replied with the same sentiment.

"I need to call my parents. Can I call you back?" I asked.

"I'll be here waiting."

"Thanks, handsome."

"Until then."

His signature reply sounded as good as the first time he said it to me. When I got in my car, I did my usual.

"Hi, baby girl! How did it go?" my dad asked.

I was smiling as I merged onto the GW Parkway.

"Hi, dad! It was great."

"Glad to hear that."

"Where's mom?"

"She's in the family room watching HGTV." He laughed.

"May I speak with her?"

"One second."

I heard him tell my mom I was on the phone.

"Hi, Sam! How was your trip?"

"Hi, mom! I had a really nice time, and Bryson was a true gentleman."

"That's great. I'm glad you're back safely. Do you think you'll see him again?"

I was still smiling and thinking about Bryson. He had asked me the same question more than once before I left Dallas. I can't lie and say I wasn't considering it.

"I'm not sure mom. We'll see what the future holds."

"Take your time. I'm not rushing you by any means."

"I know mama. Well, I just wanted to call and let you guys know I was back."

"We appreciate that."

"I'll talk to you guys in a few days. I love you guys."

"We love you too Sam."

Traffic was light. I made it to my condo quicker than usual. I didn't call Carrie, and I didn't call Bryson back. The garage attendant was his normal chipper self.

"Welcome back Ms. Hunt."

"Thank you, Mr. Pranesh."

When I got off the elevator, I could see what looked like a vase of tulips outside of my door. My first thought was William making a desperate attempt after my fatal mistake. He knew I loved tulips. No one knew I was out of town except my parents and Carrie. As I approached my door, I wondered how long they had been there. I bent down to pick up the vase and pulled out the card.

Hi Sam! It's only been a few hours since you left and I can't stop thinking about you. Bryson.

If anyone had walked by me, they would have seen a look of shame instead of joy on my face. The audacity of me to give William an ounce of credit made me feel the size of an ant. I unlocked my door and walked to my kitchen and placed the vase of tulips on my counter. I stood there feeling so ashamed. I felt a tear well up in my left eye. I needed to render myself free of William's spell over me. Even after an amazing weekend with Bryson, here I was still *expecting* efforts from the man who claimed he was in love with me but clearly was in love more with himself. Embarrassed, I muster up enough strength to call and thank you, Bryson.

"Hi, beautiful!" he said.

I felt shallow and lacking self-respect.

"Thank you for the beautiful tulips."

"You're welcome, Sam."

"They're my favorite."

"Are they really?"

"Yes! You shouldn't have."

"I'm glad you like them."

"I do."

"The message is true to the letter," he said.

I bit my bottom lip and smiled. His charm was like an addictive drug that left me craving for more at any cost.

"I had a great time Bryson and thought about you the whole flight."

Talking to him gave me life again after my shameful assumptions.

"Handsome, I would like to shower and relax. What time is your flight tomorrow?"

"No problem Sam. I leave at 9:50 AM."

"Okay, I'll call you before you take off."

"Have a good night Sam. I miss you."

I paused, then I said something I hadn't said to a man in two years.

"I miss you too, Bryson."

After we hung up, Max was now at my feet. I rubbed him before heading to my bathroom to shower. Before I stepped into the shower, I told Alexa to play Leela James *I don't want you back*. Before the first lyrics of the song, I was crying as the hot water splashed against my body. I yelled repeat to my digital assistant as the hot water mixed in with the tears; I leaned against the wall of my shower. I banged on the wall and screamed I hate you at the top of my lungs. As Leela's voice faded saying her last *I don't want you back*, I yelled at Alexa to play *living in confusion*. By the time Phyliss Hyman's sultry voice entered my steamy bathroom, I was on the floor of my shower. The hot water and tears were battling each other. I yelled obscenities and another I hate you.

Hyman's lyrics faded into silence. The water turning was warm now; I stood up and grabbed my loofah sponge to wash up. The tears were flowing less but still present. I rinsed off and stepped out of the shower. I wrapped my towel around me and sat at my vanity. My eyes were swollen and red. I turned on the cold water and splashed my face a few times. The cool feeling felt great, but it was no good for my eyes. I needed rest. I stood up and put on my robe. I stood at the entrance of my bedroom gathering my thoughts. Then I went to my chest of drawers. I didn't throw his things away. Shame on me I know. I started pulling out everything I had put in the first trash bag. I got *another* trash bag from the kitchen and put all of his junk inside then walked it to the trash chute. I stood there with the chute open and the trash bag inside, but I couldn't let go of the trash bag. The tears returned, and my grip tightened. This should have been a quick drop and back to my condo. Looking at the bag of bad memories, I wiped my eyes. I felt my grip loosen. I saw his face, his picture-perfect smile, heard his cunning tongue with the Casanova words, and thought about the fun times. My hand was just holding the yellow drawstring of the trash bag now. Then I heard that cunning tongue say, "Sam my career is important to me, and I'm moving to New York."

I released the trash bag and closed the trash chute.

When I got back to my condo, I deleted all of his contact information and blocked him from being able to contact me. In a much calmer voice, I told Alexa to play *why does it hurt so bad*. I poured a glass of Shiraz and headed to my bedroom. I lay in my bed listening to Whitney and cried some more before falling asleep.

Chapter 20

I slept so good I didn't hear my alarm. It was 9:03 AM. I had seriously overslept. I didn't see the point of going in. I sat up in my bed and saw Max in his normal spot. I looked at my nightstand and saw the almost empty glass of Shiraz. The light on my phone was blinking. I got out of bed to wash my face and brush my teeth. When I turned on the lights in my bathroom, I immediately saw my puffy eyes. I turned on the cold water and splashed it on my face. The cold water brought me to my reality.

"Bryson!"

I ran to my bedroom and grabbed my cell phone. He had called twice and left voicemails and sent a text asking if I was okay. I dialed him and started walking around in a nervous panic. His voice was so calming when he answered. I could hear the crowded airplane background noise.

"Sam, are you okay?"

I felt his sincerity and concern. I closed my eyes and exhaled. I couldn't speak immediately thinking how bad I felt assuming the recently evicted tenant had sent the beautiful tulips.

"Sam!"

"Yes!" that was all I could muster up.

"I was worried about you. I called your office as well."

"Bryson I'm sorry. I overslept this morning and didn't go into the office."

"No apology needed. Did something happen after we spoke?"

"I do owe you an apology. I told you I would call you before you took off. The boarding doors are closing soon."

"It's okay Sam."

"The last time you were boarding an airplane you didn't board in your group in order to keep talking to me."

"I wasn't on Southwest, so I didn't have a middle seat."

He made me laugh camouflaging the tear explosion brewing. His calming demeanor was soothing like a fairy tale prince charming.

"I started some early summer cleaning last night and couldn't stop."

"I don't like clutter," he said.

"Tell me about it." I laughed.

"It's good to hear you laugh Sam. It lets me know you're okay."

"Yes, I am."

I heard the flight attendant make the departure announcement. I heard me sulk because I really wanted to talk to him longer.

"I don't want to, but I have to go Sam."

I hadn't ever felt so important to someone.

"I'll make it up to you Bryson."

"You already have. Talk to you in about 9 hours."

I bit my bottom lip.

"Okay, handsome."

"Until then."

His signature goodbye.

"Bryson!"

"Yes, Sam."

I didn't say it right away. I closed my eyes and thought about the last time we kissed before I left Dallas.

"I miss you!" I said.

"I miss you more. The flight attendant is coming, I have to go," he said.

"Okay. Have a safe flight."

He whispered until then and disconnected.

I lowered my cell phone to my chest and held it there for a few moments. I sat at the countertop in my kitchen and prayed that this man was for real.

I called my boss and told a lie about not feeling well. She was more than understanding and told me to get well soon. I jumped in the shower to freshen up. I called Carrie when I finished showering to check on her.

"Good morning Sam! How was your trip?"

"Better than I expected. How are you? I was hoping to talk to you while I was gone."

"Sam you were visiting Brian, and I didn't want to be rude."

"Bryson." I laughed.

"You know what I mean," she said.

"I didn't go in today. What do you have planned?"

She didn't answer right away.

"An appointment to confirm what the first response kit told me."

"Is Jonathan going with you?"

"No, he isn't."

Her tone confirmed my thoughts on how the conversation went.

"I'll come with you, Carrie."

"Sam, you don't have to waste your day off with me."

"Are you kidding me? What time is it?" I asked.

"11:45 AM!"

"You coming to get me?"

I could hear her whimpering.

"Thank you, Sam. I'll come get you."

"It's going to be okay Carrie."

"I'll see you soon. Can we get lunch afterward?"

"Sure."

We disconnected, and I went to my closet to find something comfortable to wear. I looked at the time, and it had only been thirty minutes since Bryson's plane departed. I was missing him already. I smiled and kept getting dressed. Carrie called me and told me she was pulling up to my complex. I jumped on the elevator to meet my best friend in hopes of cheering her up. When I got off the elevator, my phone vibrated. I had a voicemail. I opened my voicemail, and the message was from a 929 area code. I didn't listen to it. I should have deleted it. The area code is from the New York City area. It was the evicted tenant. I walked up to Carrie's car and got in. I leaned in and hugged Carrie.

"Why didn't you go to work today?" she asked as she pulled off.

"I overslept."

"Oh! I thought you got back early afternoon?" she asked.

"I did."

"So what happened? That's not like you Sam."

"You wouldn't believe me if I told you."

She looked at me quickly trying not to get into an accident.

"I'll tell you all about it over lunch," I said.

"You know I can't drink."

I laughed now that I knew the reason why she couldn't drink.

"Don't worry you won't need a drink."

Carrie had been going to the same OB/GYN for years. The office was in Northwest DC. When we parked and started walking up the sidewalk, Carrie stopped walking, hugged me and cried. I held her tightly.

"Carrie we will get through this."

"I'm so scared Sam."

"I'll be right here."

"I really appreciate you."

We continued walking to her doctor's office. I wanted to ask about Jonathan but decided against it. The office wasn't busy. There were three other women months along in their pregnancy in the waiting area. I sat down as Carrie signed in. The 929 area code voicemail was eating at me. Carrie came and sat next to me.

"So tell me about your trip," she said.

I smiled.

"Wow, you smiling already?" she asked.

"I had a really nice time."

"What did you guys do?"

"We went to a speakeasy, a couple of museums, and some places to eat."

"Did you get laid?" She laughed. "Don't answer yet I have to go to the ladies' room."

"Okay."

When she left for the ladies room, I pulled out my cellphone to listen to the voicemail.

Hi Samantha, it's Will can we talk please? Why have you blocked me from calling you? Call me please.

Carrie returned from the ladies' room just as the nurse called her back for her appointment.

"Come on Sam."

I deleted the voicemail and walked back with Carrie. The nurse was very pleasant and asked her what brings her in today.

"I believe I'm pregnant," Carrie said.

The nurse continued with the standard appointment intake questions. When she finished, she told Carrie they would take blood today to confirm. I sat there holding her hand. Her doctor walked in shortly after the nurse left.

"Good afternoon Carrie. How are you feeling?" her doctor asked.

"Feeling pretty good, considering."

Her doctor smiled and spoke to me.

"Well, it looks like you're about 6 weeks pregnant. Congratulations."

I saw Carrie give a spurious smile.

"Thank you."

"Do you have any questions?"

"No."

"Okay, so we'll see you once a month until your 28th week, then it will be twice a month."

"Okay."

Carrie's tone was so low and blasé.

"I do have one question," she said.

"Sure."

Her doctor was so bubbly.

Carrie didn't say anything right away. The doctor was sitting in front of her smiling and waiting.

"How many weeks can I be should I decide to terminate the pregnancy?"

My heart sank to the floor, and I felt myself squeeze her hand. Carrie looked at me.

"Carrie, you have about three weeks."

"Thank you."

"Okay. You can set up your prenatal appointments at the front desk," she said.

Then her doctor wished us both a great day and left the room.

"Carrie!"

"Not now Sam." She stood up to leave.

When we got to the counter to check out, the receptionist asked when Carrie would like to set up her first appointment.

"I'll call you guys back. How much is my co-pay today?"

I walked into the waiting room. Carrie came out and walked right by me without saying anything. Outside she walked a few paces in front of me. I gave her some space. After all, it was her decision. She got in her car, and I heard the engine rev. That was my cue either I was riding or catching the metro back to my condo. I opened the passenger door and got in.

"Where would you like to eat?" she asked.

"Wherever you want Carrie."

She didn't say anything, just put her car in drive and proceeded to the undisclosed location. I looked out of the window in silence. She turned on Wisconsin Avenue towards Georgetown. The silence was thick as the Central Coast California fog.

"Is Cava fine?"

"Sure, Carrie."

She found street parking not too far from the restaurant. We spoke five words after hearing her sociopolitical movement question. I didn't really have an appetite.

Chapter 21

Carrie placed her order and walked to a table facing the street. I ordered a mini soup and a bottle of water then joined her by the window. I sat across from her looking out of the window, then she spoke as if a movie director said action.

"So did you get laid?" she asked.

I searched my head for a better word than irritated. But between my loss of appetite and the lingering question I drew a blank. Instead, I smiled at my hormone imbalanced friend.

"Yes."

"How was it?"

"Carrie!" Seriously?"

"Okay. Why didn't you go in today?"

She was all over the place.

"When I got home, there was a vase with tulips outside my door."

"Really?"

Some excitement finally entered her voice.

"Yes. I thought they were from William."

"Why?"

My excitement came and went that fast.

"I don't know. I thought he was up to his charming schemes."

"Who were they from? Bryson?"

She said his name right finally.

"Yes. I felt horrible."

"Rightfully so," she said.

I didn't want to go back to the silent room.

"So after I thanked Bryson, I went through my condo and bagged everything I had belonging to William."

"Did you have that much?" she asked as she scarfed her food down.

"More than I should have."

"Are you going to mail it to him?"

"Are you serious?" I asked.

"What?" she asked.

"I put it down the trash chute."

"And that's why you overslept."

"No. The night was worse than a funeral. I cried, played music, and drank wine."

"Are you done with him now? Really?" she asked.

"Yes." I thought about his voicemail.

Now it was my turn.

"Carrie! What was that about in the doctor's office?"

"Weighing my options."

"What about Jonathan?"

"What about him?"

"Did you guys talk about this?"

She didn't answer right away. I didn't realize it, but my voice had escalated a bit, and the restaurant was filling up with the lunch crowd.

"Jonathan wants to go back to school. He doesn't want this baby," she said.

"Were those his words Carrie?"

"What were William's words before you terminated your pregnancy?"

She didn't give me a chance to answer. She was in defense mode now.

"Oh that's right you didn't tell him." There it was. My justice served on a cold platter of reality. Two weeks after I broke off the engagement with William, I too had used the same first response kit brand that Carrie had used and found out I was pregnant. When I called her crying, she didn't say anything except I'll be right over, and here I was trying to steal her right to make her own decision. She never asked me any questions. She was by my side as we walked past the pro-life sign holders. I didn't tell my parents only Carrie. She basically moved in with me and put her life on hold. I regretted the decision as soon as I was released from the clinic. I was so angry and didn't want to raise a child on my own nor did I want anything else to do with William. Had I gone through with the pregnancy, that would have been a lifetime relationship with the man that chose his career over me. At that time, I didn't think I was strong enough to deal with that.

Carrie wasn't looking at me now. I lowered my head in shame.

"I'm sorry Carrie."

She kept staring out of the window and didn't acknowledge my apology.

"I don't want you to regret the decision later."

She still didn't look at me.

"Like I did," I said.

I felt her hand touch my hand. She still wasn't looking at me though. I felt the patrons of the trendy restaurant looking at us or was it just me.

"I'm sorry Sam," she said.

"It's okay. I should have been the friend you were to me."

She looked at me with tears in her eyes. I pulled a napkin from the holder and gave it to her. I knew for sure now we were center stage for the lunch crowd. Carrie wiped her face and looked around and told me, "Let's get out of here."

I needed Bryson's calming voice right now. When we got outside, Carrie said, "I feel like some ice cream."

"Ben and Jerry's here we come," I said with a smile.

Carrie smiled, and we started walking to the ice cream shop. As we walked up M Street, I didn't ask any more questions, I just enjoyed our time together. I could see Carrie browsing through the many store windows we passed. I wondered if she was really going to terminate her pregnancy. Why had Jonathan been such a jerk when she told him? I looked up at the sky and wondered how Bryson was doing, then looked at my watch to see how much longer he'd be in the friendly skies. If he took off after we hung up, he had two and a half hours left. I smiled and felt giddy inside thinking of our weekend together.

"Sam, let's go inside this store."

Carrie interrupted my daydream.

"Sure," I said.

It was a small boutique store that didn't sell maternity clothes. I hope this stop wasn't the ink sealing the deal. Inside the store, my best friend looked at skirts and tops as if she wasn't going to gain any weight at all. She actually tried on a couple of outfits and decided to buy one of them. I smiled in disappointment when she asked me how she looked. My silence was eating at the core of my soul trying not to revisit our conversation back in the restaurant. When we got back on M Street, I found myself staring at the bag Carrie was holding and having hateful thoughts wishing someone would snatch it from her and run off.

Inside the ice cream shop, there weren't any tables available and the line was at the door. I hadn't had ice cream in a minute, but I needed something sweet to calm my nerves. Carrie was oblivious to my frustration.

"Sam, what flavor are you getting?" she asked smiling.

"I don't know. What about you?"

"Two scoops of chunky monkey with hot fudge."

"That sounds good. I think I'm going to have the chocolate chip cookie dough."

As we made our way down the line, I looked around to see if someone might be leaving a table. Based on Carrie's recent purchase, I didn't feel comfortable using the prego lady plea.

"I like their chocolate chip cookie dough. Maybe I'll have that as well," Carrie said.

"You can have some of mine if you like."

"Thanks, Sam." She smiled.

We placed our order, and Carrie paid for my ice cream. When we turned around, an older gentleman sitting at a table alone offered us his table. We both smiled and thanked him. Carrie pulled out her cell phone for the first time all day. I saw her face frown, and then I heard her say under her breath, "Yeah whatever" followed by some vulgar words.

"Is everything okay?" I asked.

"Yes. Just Jonathan texting me asking if we can talk."

I didn't know what to say without being judgmental again. The old saying if you don't have anything good to say then don't say anything at all clamped my lips shut. Carrie put a spoonful of ice cream in her mouth and savored it.

"Sam, I'm sorry about earlier."

"It's okay girl. I had no right-"

She cut me off before I finished my sentence.

"Sure you did. I'm just so angry at myself."

"Why? I thought you and Jonathan were a great couple."

"Not to sound cliché but if we were, then he wouldn't have reacted the way he did when I told him I was pregnant," she said.

"It will be okay Carrie one way or the other, and you know I'm here for you."

She touched my hand and smiled.

"I know Sam."

We sat and enjoyed our ice cream and forgot all about the earlier contentious moments. Afterward we walked back to Carrie's car. I could tell she was getting tired. Her body was going through changes whether she liked it or not. I suggested that we end our day. She agreed and took me home. When we pulled up in front of my building, Carrie put her car in park.

"Sam, can I ask you something?"

"Sure, what is it?"

"Do you really regret your decision?"

I looked out of the window replaying that day in my mind. I felt empty. I felt stupid for allowing William to have such an influence still on my life that I made such a horrible decision. I knew my parents wanted grandkids. I'm sure they would have gotten over me being an unwed mother.

"Everyday! But you have to do what you feel is best for you."

I smiled and said goodbye opening the passenger car door. Bryson should be landing soon, and I could hardly wait to tell him how much I missed him and to hear how much he missed me. Carrie didn't say anything before I closed the door. I leaned down and peeked through the passenger window. We made eye contact and silently said I love you.

Chapter 22

I felt exhausted and needed a shower. I let my bathroom get steamy before entering the shower. The truth is, I was hoping Bryson would call. The steaming hot water felt so good that I let it rinse away the bad memories of the afternoon with Carrie. In the midst of my selfish emotions, I crossed the line I shouldn't have. I really hoped our apologies were sincere and that we would move on from this. I made myself a promise that I would support Carrie regardless of her decision. I finished my shower and put on a pair of shorts and t-shirt. I noticed the extra space in a few of my drawers since I had gotten rid of some old things. I walked into the kitchen to get a glass of wine. I checked my phone and Bryson had called and left a voicemail. I called him right back without listening to his voicemail.

"Hi, Sam!"

His voice immediately made me high.

"Hi, handsome. How was your flight?"

"It was long and I missed you."

"Oh stop. You've made that flight many times."

"Yes I have, but I've never gotten on the plane with someone on my mind as much as you were."

"What about your ex-girlfriend?"

"It wasn't like this."

"Are you home?"

"No, I'm driving now."

"How far are you from the airport?"

"Maybe 40 minutes. What have you been doing since we last spoke."

I sat down on one of my bar stools and took a sip of my wine.

"I spent most of the day with my best friend."

"How was that? What is her name by the way?"

"It ended well, but there were some rough moments."

"Sorry to hear that. You want to talk about it?"

"I'm sure you don't want to hear all of that. But thank you."

"Sam, give me the short version then. Best friends don't come every day."

There was that charm of his. I wasn't sure I wanted to share Carrie's personal business with him. I took another sip of my wine and looked out of my big window.

"Bryson, I said something to her that I shouldn't have basically."

"Did you apologize?" he asked.

I felt defensive from his question. He didn't even know the specifics, and it felt like he was on Carrie's side. I moved to the couch with my wine.

"Yes, I did," I said flatly.

"What's wrong Sam?"

He could tell my tone had changed.

"I'm fine. We will work it out."

He didn't say anything right away.

"I miss you too much to argue Sam."

"We're fine. We barely know each other."

"Ouch!"

I didn't say anything, and neither did he. 48 hours ago it felt magical being with him, and his one question turned the whole conversation. That was the perfect indicator for me to slow this thing down we'd started.

"Well, Bryson I'm sure you're tired and want to get home and settled."

"Wow! It's like that Samantha?"

He called me by my full name and in a cold, hurtful tone. His love meter was downshifting as well.

"Bryson, I'm tired, and I'm glad you made it back to Germany safely."

"Thanks for your hallmark card sentiment."

"I shouldn't have brought up my situation with Carrie. It wasn't fair to you."

"Don't patronize me. Enjoy the rest of your evening. Goodbye!"

"Okay, Bryson."

He hung up without saying 'until then.' I had gotten used to him saying that. I sat there thinking about what just happened. I had to smile to myself because technically we weren't in a relationship and we just had a little tiff. I thought about calling him back and apologizing. I pulled up his contact profile, but the slight buzz I was feeling wouldn't allow me to push the button. I smiled again and finished my glass of wine before turning in.

I woke up the next morning with a slight headache, but I couldn't miss another day of work. I checked my cell phone and saw that Bryson had called back a few times but didn't leave a message. I showered and headed into the office. Guilt got the best of me during my drive in. I'd over-reacted to something that was really my fault. I sat in my parking space thinking about Bryson and realized the way I treated him was how William had treated me many times. I had always heard if you hung around people long enough you would develop some of their behaviors. My snappy behavior was classic William and unfair to Bryson.

I utilized the international calling plan I had signed up for.

"DHS Frankfurt branch"

"Hi"

"Sam?"

"I'm sorry!"

There was a brief silence before Bryson spoke.

"It's okay Sam. I shouldn't have voiced my opinion without asking more about the situation."

His charm was on duty 24/7.

"No it's my fault and I wanted to call you to apologize."

"Sam."

I loved the way he said my name. I immediately felt better, and my headache was gone.

"Yes."

"I miss you, and I don't want to fight like that again."

"Me either."

"Do you miss me, Sam?"

"More than you could imagine."

"Can I come see you?"

"When? You just got back?"

"For my birthday in a couple of months."

"You sure you want to spend your special day with me?"

"I wouldn't want to spend it with anyone else."

"Sure."

"I will get a hotel room."

"For what, silly? You wasted money on the two bedrooms in Dallas." I laughed.

He laughed before he responded.

"True."

"Well let me know the days so I can put in to be off. How many days are you coming for?"

"How long can I stay?"

"Is five days long enough?"

"No, but okay."

"How long did you want to stay?"

"Sam"

"Yes."

"Do you believe in love at first sight?"

I was afraid to answer that question honestly because love, at first sight, got me hurt, pregnant and unwed. I stalled before answering.

"Why do you ask?"

"That's how I felt during my briefing in Orlando."

"I didn't think you noticed me."

"You didn't think I was smiling at your supervisor, did you?"

I laughed.

"When I saw you, I knew I was destined to make you mine," he said.

I was blushing and lost track of time. The parking lot had filled with more cars.

"Bryson I'm still sitting in my car, and I need to get upstairs."

"Is that a no to my question?"

I looked in the rearview mirror at myself. "Yes, I do." I exhaled.

"Okay, I will let you get into the office. Talk to you soon."

"Again, I'm sorry for last night."

"It's okay Sam."

Then his signature farewell returned.

"Until then."

I smiled as the international call fell silent.

I got out of my car and entered the building smiling and feeling alive ready to take on the cyber world.

Chapter 23

Bryson and I continued to communicate every day over the phone and email and talked about him visiting me. I got used to the time difference and was able to time my calls just right. I learned his daily routine. He got up early and jogged daily before going into the office. He also worked out at one of the local gyms four or five times a week. On the weekends, he didn't do much. He told me about a few colleagues he met for drinks and played golf with on occasion. I told him my daily and weekend routines as well. I eventually told him about the contentious moment Carrie and I had. As always he was comforting and told me to cherish real friendships because they are hard to find these days. I agreed with him.

Carrie and I hung out quite a bit. We set up a baby register at her favorite stores and never spoke of what happened at her first appointment again. I took off and attended all of her appointments with her. Jonathan disappeared after she told him she was keeping the baby and stopped wanting to have sex with her. I had been receiving random calls from numbers I didn't recognize, and the caller never left a message. One evening while driving home, they called repeatedly, and it annoyed me to the point I answered.

"HELLO!"

"Sam."

A low whimpering voice I didn't recognize said my name. I turned up the Bluetooth volume and said hello again.

"Sam it's me."
"William?"
"Yes."
I slowed my speed.
"What do you want?" I asked annoyed.
"Why have you blocked me from calling you?"
"That should be obvious. What do you want?"

The tension was building, and my grip on the steering wheel tightened.

"I miss you," he said.

Even his whimpering voice affected me. I got myself together quickly though. I couldn't fall for his empty promises anymore.

"Don't say that to me."
"I do really."

It sounded like he was crying.

"William, we don't have anything to talk about."
"Please don't say that Sam. Can we try again?" he asked.
"Try what? Wasting each other's time? Oh no, I meant can we have sex again?"
"Sam, please! This isn't about sex."
"What is it about then? Don't you think you've hurt me enough?"
Silence.
"I'm sorry Sam."

The tears and sobbing confirmed he was crying.

"William I don't know what crisis you're dealing with, but I hope you get through it. I need to go."

Silence and the sounds of sobbing continued from the other end.

"William!" I said.
"Yes."

My best attempt to be stern with the man who'd left me wasn't worth two pennies.

"What's wrong?" I asked.

"Sam, I know I messed up, but I need you back," he said.

I heard him sniffle. I remained silent and mad at myself.

"I know I shouldn't have moved to New York and left you."

"You made the best decision for yourself at the time."

"No. It was selfish."

"William…"

My phone beeped. It was Bryson. He had started calling me before he went to bed. I listened to the incoming call beep a few more times.

"Sam, please give us another chance," he pleaded.

The incoming call beeps stopped. Damn what's wrong with me?

"William I really need to go."

"Will you at least think about what I said?" he asked.

"You haven't said anything."

"Sam, I said a lot."

"You said the same things you've said in the past with no follow through."

"This time it's different," he said.

"I've heard that before too."

"I mean it this time. I'll even move back to DC."

"William you don't mean any of this. All of what you said sounded good, and it tricked me into believing you. Not this time."

"I'm serious Sam!"

Bryson was calling again.

"Goodbye William and please stop calling me."

I heard him saying something as I disconnected the call. I dialed Bryson back. He answered on the second ring.

"Hi, there! Is everything okay?" he asked.

"Yes. I was on the other line with my parents. Sorry."

I lied and felt bad.

"Oh okay, no problem. I was just heading to bed and wanted to say good night."

His voice sounded so sincere. We hadn't missed a night of saying good night, and I had gotten used to talking to him on my way home.

"I know handsome. Are you in bed?"

"Yes. How long before you get home?" he asked.

"Just a few more minutes. I won't keep you. We can talk in the morning."

"Okay please send me a text to let me know you've made it home safe."

"I will do that."

"I miss you and can't wait to see you."

"I miss you too. Not much longer."

"Until then."

I parked my car in the garage of my condo building but didn't get out of my car right away. My mind replayed the conversation with William. He had never cried over anything in all the years I'd known him. His past attempts of rekindling our relationship were arrogant followed by saying the right things to hypnotize me over to his hotel room. I got out of my car and headed upstairs. Max was in his favorite spot. I sent Bryson a text to let him know I was home. He replied immediately with a thank you. I poured myself a glass of wine and stared in Max's direction at the city lights of DC. I let the past take me captive thinking of the good times William and I had and tried to justify the bad ones. Three glasses of wine later I found myself trying to remember the number I deleted from my cell phone. I slammed the phone down in frustration. I poured another glass of wine and tried to remember those ten deadly digits. The number I dialed began to ring. I slapped the countertop as I sipped my wine. The silver tongue devil didn't answer. His sexy soothing voicemail captured my drunken message.

I miss you. Why did you do this to us? Did you mean the things you said earlier? Did you? Oh William, William.

I hung up and finished my wine then took a shower. I checked my phone when I got out of the shower. No missed calls. I crawled into my bed and cried myself to sleep.

Chapter 24

My alarm woke me up from a deep sleep. I pressed snooze for ten minutes. Bryson called before the snooze alerted me.

"Good morning beautiful."

I didn't feel that way at all.

"Good afternoon," I said.

"I thought you'd be up."

He was chipper and sounded happy to hear my voice. My thoughts were in a tailspin and not in the happy zone he was in. I sat up and forced an enthusiastic response.

"Handsome I'm up, just moving slow. I had some wine last night."

"Oh, okay. We can catch up later if you want."

"No, it's fine. Your day is almost over. How was it?"

"It was productive. We had to deal with a couple of potential hacks," he said.

"Oh sorry."

"That's what I get paid for." He laughed.

"Not much longer until we see each other," I said smiling.

"Yes. Are you excited like I am?"

My bad feelings returned. This man was clearly all about me, yet I was calling the man who'd hurt me more than I wanted to remember leaving drunken messages and checking to see if he called me back. I threw my pillow off the bed.

"Yes, I can't wait."

"Well Sam get up, and we'll talk soon."

I didn't want to hang up. I needed him to save me from myself. I was afraid I'd redial those devil laced digits.

"Okay. I'll email you when I get in the office."

"Sounds good."

"Talk to you soon, handsome."

"Until then." He hung up.

I got up and took another shower before heading into the office. On the way in, I called the person I knew could put me back on track.

"Good morning."

"Hi, dad."

"How are you?"

"I'm fine."

"Uh, oh. I know you better than you know yourself. What's wrong?"

"William called," I said.

"Sam, I hope you were cordial."

I couldn't remember ever hearing my father raise his voice or get upset. Even when I called him crying my eyeballs out when William left me, he was so calm and told me not to worry, and everything would be okay.

"No, I wasn't but then."

"Then what, Sam?"

"Dad I thought I was over him."

"Aren't you? I thought you were as well."

"He asked me to give him another chance."

"What did you tell him?"

"I told him to stop calling me."

"Sam it's your decision, but that's a dangerous road to travel again."

"Dad I know but I still."

"I know you still love him. You may love him for the rest of your life. But you can't let him use love as your emotional kryptonite."

The tears started to roll down my face. It was as if my dad heard William's tantalizing tongue last night and knew how close I was to committing a huge mistake.

"I know, dad. I guess I just needed to hear it from you."

"You're an intelligent woman. You don't need my $.02." He laughed.

"Your word is priceless. I love you."

"I love you, too."

"Thank you. I need to get into the office. Tell mom I will call her later."

"I will do that. Stay strong."

"Okay, daddy."

When I pulled into the building parking lot, I felt so much better and knew I'd have a great day. I emailed Bryson when I logged in, and we talked the rest of the morning until he left his office. By then, it was lunchtime for me. I went downstairs to the cafeteria to grab something to eat. On my way back upstairs, the security guard got my attention.

"Ms. Hunt another delivery."

I smiled and approached the counter.

"Thank you."

"You're welcome."

I blushed and walked to the elevator. On the elevator, I pulled out the card from the beautiful bouquet of red roses. I started reading the card and felt like the elevator was descending into hell. The flowers were from William. This was his cowardly way of responding to my drunken message. When I got off the elevator, I walked as quickly as I could to the break room and threw the flowers away and stopped by the shredder room to dispose of the meaningless card. I was fuming mad at myself for calling him last night and furious at his 1-800flowers.com efforts. I wasn't worth a return call, but I'd ignored Bryson's call twice while listening to his bogus tears. I walked into my office and slammed my door. I sat at my desk thinking of the things he said last night and started crying knowing I was actually considering his empty promises once again. I heard a light tap on my door. I wiped my eyes before answering.

"Yes."

"Ms. Hunt, you okay?"

It was my supervisor.

"Yes, I'm fine. Thanks."

"I'm here if you want to talk about it."

"Thank you, but I'm fine, really."

"Okay."

I heard her walk away. I grabbed my cell phone and dialed William's number. His voice answered full of glee.

"Hi, Sam!"

"William, this has to stop!"

The glee disappeared instantly.

"What are you talking about?" he asked, playing coy.

"William I'm not giving you another chance."

"It didn't sound that way last night."

His arrogance was back.

"Charge it to the wine I was drinking. We are done."

"You don't mean that," he said.

His charm was battling with my emotional strength, and I was losing. Stay strong Sam.

"I mean it. You've played with my heart long enough."

"Sam, I apologized. I really meant what I said."
"I'm sure you did. It's just too late, William."
"Too late? Are you seeing someone?"
Here was my chance to stick the dagger in. Go for it, Sam.
"That's none of your business."
Coward.
"Sam please don't do this."
"William."
"Yes!"
"Are you listening?"
"Yes, Sam."
I could tell he was smiling.
"We are done. Get lost and don't waste your time or mine calling me from random numbers!"
"Sam!"
Click.

I sat at my desk and enjoyed my Cobb salad and sparkling water. I finished my day with a sense of accomplishment. William called my desk a few more times but didn't leave a message.

My evening drive home was like it had been the past weeks. I smiled all the way home. I called my mommy, and we talked for a little while until I got sleepy. I didn't have any wine before going to bed.

Chapter 25

The next couple of weeks flew by. Carrie's pregnancy was moving along without any complications. Bryson was arriving this afternoon, and I was a little nervous. I checked the departure and arrival board at Reagan National airport to see if his flight was on time. The display board showed an on time arrival. I had butterflies in my stomach waiting for him. I called Carrie.

"Is he here?" she asked excitedly.

"His flight lands any minute now."

"Great! How are you feeling?" she asked.

"Nervous for some reason."

"Why? You guys have seen each other already."

"I know, but I haven't had a man in a place since you know who."

"Anyway Sam. You will be fine."

"Sorry I won't be at your appointment next week," I said.

"It's okay. I'll text you and let you know how it goes."

"Thanks. I see him walking. I'll talk to you later."

"Okay, have fun, Sam."

"Will do, bye."

Bryson approached me smiling, casually dressed and looking handsome. He had a carry-on and a messenger bag over his shoulder. I felt giddy and ran the short distance to him and hugged him.

"I guess you missed me," he said.

I held him tight and exhaled.

"Yes, I did. You smell good."

He kissed me and said, "I missed you more."

"Is that all of your luggage?" I asked.

"Yes, I think I over packed." He laughed.

"Are you hungry?" I asked.

"A little."

"What do you have a taste for?" I asked.

"Anything except a chain restaurant."

"Okay, we'll head into the city then."

"Lead the way," he said.

He grabbed my hand and pulled me in for another kiss. His lips were so soft, and the way he kissed me was like no one had ever kissed me before. We slowly made our way to the parking garage. When we got to the machine, he offered to pay the parking fee. I smiled at him and told him he was a guest. The drive into the city wasn't bad, and luckily none of the streets were blocked off for a major event. He cracked his windows and let some fresh air hit him.

"So where are you taking me?" he asked.

"Claudia's in Northwest."

"Is it good?"

"I've never been. I've heard it is."

"Another first for us." He smiled.

I looked at him and smiled. Someone else would have had an attitude. Stop it Sam.

"Thank you for taking off Sam."

"Of course!"

"So what do you have planned?"

"Wait and see, Mister."

I got lucky and found parking on the street.

Claudia's didn't disappoint us at all. We ordered from the lunch menu. The atmosphere was laid back, and I could tell it was a romantic setting during dinner.

"Are you tired?" I asked.

"Not really. I would like to stay up as long as possible."

"Do you want to walk around the National Mall?"

"Sure, sounds good," he said.

The weather wasn't too humid, and there were a fair number of people out enjoying the sights and the history of America. Bryson took a few pictures of the buildings and of us being silly. We held hands and laughed and talked about things and places we liked. I knew talking to him over the telephone came easily, but it was even better in person. The way he talked to me was calming. He didn't make me feel rushed or like he was annoyed. There was one thing annoying me though. His cell phone kept beeping and ringing. He didn't take any of the calls or reply to any of the messages, and I tried my best not to say anything because it could have been the office in Germany. Then he blurted out, "Seriously!"

"Is everything okay, Bryson?" I asked.

"Yes."

His phone rang again. He pulled out his phone and just stared at the screen. The ringtone wasn't aggravating, but I could tell he was upset.

"Why don't you just answer it?" I said.

"I don't have anything to say to the person."

"Well, obviously they want to talk to you."

I was trying not to let this overshadow our time. I was concerned.

"Just take the call, Bryson." I walked away.

"No Sam, wait."

"It's fine."

"No, it's not. I should have handled this before I left Germany."

"Handle what?"

"It's my ex-girlfriend."

"Are you sure you two aren't together?" Now I had an attitude.

"Yes, I'm sure, Sam. I'll just turn my phone off."

"Is that the answer?"

He looked at me in a mean way. Then he looked away with his phone still in his hand. I walked away to give him some time. When I got a few feet away, I sent Carrie a text message and told her the afternoon is taking a bad turn. I looked over at Bryson, and he was typing something on his phone. When he finished, he walked over to me. He smiled at me, and I saw one of his dimples.

"Sam, I apologize, and hopefully my phone won't ring like that again."

"Okay."

"That's it?"

"Yes. I just want you to enjoy your birthday trip."

"I told my ex I was visiting my girlfriend and not to contact me anymore."

"No, you didn't Bryson." He called my bluff and pulled out his phone to show me the message. He had sent what he said, and she replied with 'she's not me but enjoy yourself if you can.' I smiled inside. "When did I become your girlfriend?" I asked and smiled.

"The moment I saw you in Orlando." He reached for my hand and directed us towards the Reflecting Pond.

Although we were holding hands, our walk started off quiet and unattached. I wanted to tell him I was fine and that he didn't have to send that text message. In my mind, we hadn't discussed being exclusive, so it wasn't a big deal. Halfway to the Lincoln Memorial, Bryson stopped walking.

"Are you tired? We can go so you can get some rest," I said.

"No, I'm fine. I want to ask you a question."

"Sure."

He looked towards the Lincoln Memorial then back at me. He grabbed the sides of my face, and I felt him massaging the place behind my ears. Then he came in to kiss me.

"Sam, will you be my girlfriend?"

It felt like we were in high school standing in the hallway just before the next class period. The attractive jock was asking the bookworm to go steady. Our eyes didn't blink, and it was as if no one else was there. I lost the staring contest when I blinked and smiled.

"Bryson are you sure you're ready?"

"Positive."

"You aren't just asking because of what happened a few minutes ago are you?"

"Sam I could have asked you the first time we spoke on the phone."

"What about the distance?"

"We'll make it work."

"How?"

"We'll book flights in advance and meet in different places as often as we can."

"For how long?" I asked.

"I have two years left, or I can apply for a curtailment."

I softly punched him in the arm.

"I'm not asking you to do that, silly."

"You don't have to," he said.

I'd never been in a long-distance relationship before but had heard the horror stories. This would take great effort and an enormous amount of trust. What would I do the nights I needed to be held? What would I do when I wanted companionship? All of that would be done through cyber efforts. It felt like time had stopped as Bryson stood there waiting for my answer. He was now rubbing the sides of my arms and smiling. He was so easy on the eyes. It was time for me to leave my comfort zone and try something new.

"Yes!"

He lifted me into the air and spun me around.

"You won't regret your decision."

"I believe you."

We continued walking towards the Lincoln Memorial. Our interlaced fingers felt more intimate than before. After reading the writings on the walls and taking more pictures, we headed to my condo.

When we walked into my condo, Max came out of the room faster than I've ever seen him do. He stared at Bryson for a few moments before coming towards me.

"I didn't know you had a cat," Bryson said.

"I've had Maxwell since he was a little kitten."

"Do you mind if I take a shower and freshen up?" he asked.

"Sure. Right this way." I hesitated briefly thinking I should take him to my guest bathroom.

"This is the master bath. Don't mind all of my stuff on the counter."

"You're funny, Sam," he said.

I got him some towels and left him to shower. A few minutes after I heard the shower, Bryson appeared before me wearing just a pair of shorts.

"Sam, will you join me in the shower?"

I stood there biting my bottom lip taking in his hot body.

"Sam," he softly called my name snapping me out of my lust filled stare.

"Yes," I said.

"Will you?" he asked.

I didn't answer and started walking towards him. Inside the shower where I'd last cried a river Bryson caressed me softly and tenderly. I immediately felt like pottery in the beginning stages of being formed. He reached for my loofah sponge and kissed me.

"Which body wash would you like?" he asked.

I stood there mesmerized, watching the water splash onto his body. I couldn't speak. I kissed him back and let my tongue dance with his. I rubbed his shoulders and squeezed his arms. His hands made their way to my spine and back, and I felt him slowly lift me up against the wall of my shower. The water splashed in our faces as I felt his lips kiss my right cheek, then my neck and the middle of my chest. The aquatic foreplay was turning me on. I felt his manhood nudge against me. He was hard and ready. I saw him look down and then back up at me. His strength held me firmly as he let me down. I saw him grab the Carol's Daughter's Ecstasy body wash. He slowly turned me around and began washing my back. I rested my hands against my shower wall. Bryson's touch coupled with the hot water felt incredibly relaxing. He came close, and I felt his hardware rub against my ass. He knelt and washed the back of my thighs down to my feet. When he stood up, he turned me around and washed under my neck down the front side of my body. I took his washcloth and applied the manly scented body wash he had. I didn't know if he was flexing his muscles as I washed him but his body was so tight. The definition in his back looked like a page torn out of the latest muscle magazine, and his ass was the best I'd ever seen. Not that I'd seen many.

We dried each other off and kissed some more. Bryson lifted me up and took me to my bed.

"I'm so happy to be here, Sam."

I smiled. "I'm glad you came."

"Thank you for having me."

"Of course, silly."

He smiled, kissed me, and lay next to me holding me. In the background, I could hear the water dripping from the shower. I felt amazing, and the way Bryson held me made me feel loved.

Chapter 26

I felt Bryson jerking then I heard him talking angrily to himself. I couldn't make out what he was saying, but it sounded like he was arguing with someone. I slid from underneath his arm and put on my shorts. I stood there trying to decide if I should wake him up or leave him to whatever nightmare was torturing him. His one-sided conversation went on for another three minutes before he fell quietly asleep. I was hesitant to get back in bed.

When Bryson woke up, I was already awake and having a cup of hot tea. I decided to sleep on my couch the few hours left before I got up.

"Good morning Sam."

"Happy Birthday, handsome. How did you sleep?"

"Thank you. I slept like a rock."

"You tossed and turned around 3 o'clock."

He didn't respond immediately.

"I did? Was I talking in my sleep?"

"Yes, you were. You sounded mad, actually."

"Mad?" He scratched his head.

"Yes. I couldn't make out everything. But I did hear you say stop and let me go."

"Oh wow. I apologize Sam."

"It's okay. I was worried about you."

"Let me go brush my teeth. Can I get a cup of hot tea please?"

"Sure."

"Be right back."

"Two minutes top and bottom," I said and laughed.

"You're funny," he said.

Bryson returned to the kitchen and kissed me before sipping his tea.

"I didn't add sugar or milk," I said.

"It tastes fine. Thank you."

"So, are you ready for a full day?" I asked.

"Of course! What are we doing?"

"You'll see. I'm going to shower."

I left him in the kitchen hoping he wouldn't join me in the shower. Last night's sleep intrusion was still on my mind, but I didn't want to push the issue on his birthday.

The hot water felt so good. I thought about my birthday plans for him and wondered if I had planned too much. I will go with his flow and scale things back if I feel it's too much. I heard my bathroom door open and could see Bryson moving around. He was getting his toiletries. He didn't join me in the shower. When I finished, I could hear the shower in my guest bathroom. I dried off and wrapped the towel around myself. Bryson had already laid out a pair of khaki cargo shorts and a light blue polo. I picked out a white pair of capris and a light yellow blouse. I heard the shower water end in my guest bathroom. Bryson walked in with his towel around his waist and smelling manly fresh. He came over and kissed me.

"Do you want me to iron your clothes?" I asked.

"Sure, if you don't mind," he said.

"Do you want to grab breakfast?" I asked.

"I'm not starving. What are we doing today?"

"Our first stop is George Washington's house in Mount Vernon."

"Great! I'll be okay until lunch then."

"You sure? We can pick up something light."

"Sounds like you're hungry," he said and laughed.

"No, I'm fine, silly."

"Okay, we can grab lunch afterward."

Bryson sat on my bed and checked his cell phone. I saw him typing quickly.

"Is everything okay?" I asked.

"Yes! Replying to some work emails."

I wondered if it was work or was his ex-girlfriend still on a rant. I finished ironing our clothes in silence. I saw Bryson look at me, but I didn't say anything. I went into my bathroom to get dressed. I applied some eyeliner and sprayed some Miss Dior on. When I turned around, Bryson was standing in the door.

"Sam, let's talk."

I turned around slowly and forced a smile. "About what? Birthday boy."

He smiled, then quickly returned to a straight face. "About me talking in my sleep," he said.

"It's not a big deal. I'm sure I have bad night in my sleep," I said.

"Not this kind and not as often," he said and lowered his head.

I walked over to him and lifted his head. "Bryson, what are you talking about?"

"Do you remember me mentioning my Aunt Gladys?"

"Yes. You said she and your Uncle Raymond helped your mother."

"Well, Gladys did more damage than helping."

"What do you mean?"

"Oh come on, Sam. Do I have to spell it out for you?"

His voice was louder and his face displayed a look of pain instead of sadness. I gently grabbed Bryson's hand and walked towards my bed and sat down.

"Bryson, if you don't want to discuss this now we don't have to. I really don't know what you're talking about."

He pulled his hand away from mine and buried his face in his hands. I touched his shoulder, and he shrugged it away and stood up. Now I was getting worried. When he turned around, I saw a look on his face that I'd never seen or imagined. "Bryson!"

He didn't respond, but I could hear him fuming.

"Bryson talk to me."

Still nothing.

"Bryson if you don't talk then I think you should leave and we forget this whole thing because I'm getting scared." More silence. I stood up and looked around for my phone in case I needed to call 911. Then he yelled out loud.

"She molested me for years!" His fists were balled up like he was ready to fight.

I was frozen and couldn't believe what I just heard. He was walking around in circles mumbling. Then he yelled again.

"For years! And no one would believe me."

"Bryson it's okay," I said.

He waved me off, and I could see he was starting to cry now.

"She did it repeatedly. I hated going to their house," he said.

"Baby, sit down."

His bitter look at me told me he didn't want to sit down. I sat down and rested my hands on the side of my face. I didn't know what to say, but I ruled out calling 911.

"That's why I don't know how to love anyone," he said.

"Bryson, that's not true. You're a wonderful man."

"Don't patronize me, Sam!" he yelled.

"Bryson please calm down and stop yelling."

"Or what? You're going to leave me like all the others. Go ahead then."

"Bryson no one's leaving. But you need to calm down. It's your birthday."

"Gladys made sure I got a nice birthday gift too."

"I'm not Gladys, and you don't have to deal with that anymore."

"I just dealt with it last night according to you."

"Bryson it's your birthday. Let's get out of here and get some fresh air."

"You sure you still want to hang out with me? I don't need your pity, Sam."

His question was indeed valid. I wasn't sure, but I didn't want him upset on his birthday. I avoided giving him a hurtful answer. I approached him cautiously, and when I felt it was safe, I hugged him. He didn't hug me back immediately. I could feel his heartbeat racing record speed. I squeezed him tighter and whispered that everything would be okay. A few seconds passed then I felt his arms fold around me.

"I'm so sorry, Sam, for the outburst and for yelling at you."

"It's okay. I just want you to enjoy your birthday."

His eyes were red from his angry tears. I wiped his eyes with the back of my hands. "Come on handsome."

I saw him form a small smile as we left my bedroom and headed towards the door to leave. As we walked to the elevator, Bryson held my hand as if I was his lifeline. When we got on the elevator, he pulled me into him and kissed me passionately like he did in Dallas.

"I'm really sorry, Sam. Can you forgive me?"

"There's nothing to forgive. Let's enjoy the rest of the day."

"Thank you," he said.

"You're welcome."

As the elevator descended to the parking garage, I felt numb, but I didn't want his birthday to be a disappointment. Both of us needed some fresh air. The drive to Mount Vernon was quiet, but our hands were interlocked, and we occasionally smiled at each other.

Chapter 27

After I picked up the tickets to begin the tour of the first President's house, I decided to follow Bryson's lead. He was much better than he was back in my condo but still not the happy, upbeat Bryson that I was used to. We started the tour with four other people. Bryson held my hand and smiled at me throughout the tour. We took selfies and made silly faces with the Potomac in the background. He seemed to be enjoying himself. When we got to the gift shop, he bought one of the many books available about George Washington.

"Thank you, Sam. This was great."

"You're welcome. Are you ready to eat lunch?" I asked.

"Sure that sounds good."

"Okay. We'll head over to the National Harbor."

"I'm following you, my lady."

When we arrived at the Harbor, the traffic was horrific and moving at a snail's pace. Bryson must have felt my impatience.

"Sam it's okay. I'm having a great time, and there's no rush."

I smiled at him. I didn't get so lucky with street parking today. We parked in one of the garages and walked to Redstone American Grill. The hostess sat us at a table facing the Potomac. It was a beautiful day, and a lot of people were enjoying the weather. Despite how Bryson's day started, I really hoped he was having a good time. He was leaving in a couple of days, and I wanted our time together to be as great as possible.

We finished our lunch and stepped outside to walk around for a while. Bryson hugged me from behind and kissed me on my cheek.

"This has been the greatest birthday ever, Sam."

"Oh come on. I doubt that."

"Seriously it has. Everything was perfect," he said.

"Do you feel like some ice cream?" I asked.

"Sure. This is a really nice area."

As we walked by the Awakening statue, I thought I heard a familiar voice call my name. I kept walking, and I didn't think Bryson heard it. The voice called for me once more.

"Is someone calling your name?" Bryson asked.

He had heard the same voice I did. It was unfamiliar to him but very familiar to me. I turned around to see William with two other guys.

"I thought that was you," William said.

"Hi, William," I said.

Bryson was holding my hand, and I could see him looking directly at William. Bryson was slightly taller and more muscular than William.

"William, this is my boyfriend, Bryson."

William extended his hand towards Bryson. I wondered if Bryson would shake his hand the way he shook mine in Orlando. Who was I kidding; there was too much male testosterone in the air. I saw the two men grip each other's hand strong, both resisting any urge to show weakness.

"So how are you, Samantha?" William asked.

Bryson was so calm. I was hoping the arrogant William wasn't present. I wasn't sure how I would react if I ever ran into William while I was with another man. I was so nervous standing there.

"I'm doing well, and yourself?" I asked.

"Things are great. I'm back in DC now. The last time we talked I told you I was moving back."

I looked at Bryson, but he was looking around the Harbor contently holding my hand.

"Good for you. Well, it was nice seeing you. Take care," I said.

"You too Sam. Take care bro."

Bryson didn't respond. When we got a few paces away, I felt my palms getting sweaty and my heart racing. I had to say something to Bryson. "That was awkward. Sorry, Bryson."

"Sorry for what?" he calmly asked.

"Of all the people I didn't think I'd run into my ex-fiancé."

Bryson laughed. "It's okay. He's a funny dude."

"Yes, he is." I laughed.

We sat inside Ben & Jerry's and ate our ice cream laughing and people-watching. We both liked chocolate, so we shared a little of each other's ice cream. Bryson didn't mention William, but I had prepared myself to be brutally honest if he asked when was the last time I'd spoken to William. After we finished our ice cream, Bryson made a joke.

"Should we walk around some more and chance running into more of your past?" he said laughing.

I punched him lightly on his arm. "Sure, fool, we can walk around some more. Who might we run into walking the streets of Germany?" I asked.

"Come visit and find out," he said.

"You're funny."

"So are you Samantha."

He was mimicking William now.

We walked down by the yachts then over to the giant Ferris wheel.

"Have you ever been on this?" Bryson asked.

"Once with Carrie."

"Let's get on and make a wish."

"Are you serious?"

"Yes, I am."

"Sure."

We got inside, and Bryson said, "We can't make the wish until we're at the very top of the wheel."

"Okay," I said.

When we got to the top, Bryson kissed me and said, "Now make your wish." I saw him close his eyes and smile. I closed my eyes and thought about what I wanted to wish for. The Wheel began to move again.

"Did you make your wish, Sam?" Bryson asked.

"Yes, I did. Did you?

He smiled. "I sure did."

When we got off the wheel, we walked around and looked at some of the boutique shops then left the Harbor. When we got back to my condo, we took showers and relaxed. I had signed us up for a wine and paint event, but we were both tired. We ordered takeout from Bangkok Joe's and watched George Lopez live from the Kennedy on Netflix. I opened a bottle of Shiraz, and we laughed until tears were in our eyes. When the show was over, Bryson took our plates to the kitchen, cleaned up, and put the leftovers in my refrigerator. I went to the bathroom to floss and brush my teeth. Bryson joined me and when I was done, he lifted me up and took me to my bedroom. He gently laid me on my bed and began kissing me. I felt his hands caressing my body softly. His kisses were erotic, and the way he squeezed me left me in a relaxed state. He lifted my t-shirt over my head and slid my shorts down my legs. He kissed my body, and I felt his warm breath on my skin. My body was on fire from his mesmerizing touches. I saw him take his shirt and shorts off. I felt his body touch mine, and soon I felt him slide inside of me. He didn't put on a condom, and I didn't protest. The trust of exclusivity silently implied I suppose. The way Bryson made love to me was amazing. Our moans battled to stay in rhythm. He had one of my legs on his shoulders and the passion I felt made me forget we ran into William. Made me wish I could have Bryson's loving every day. Made me wish I were Mrs. Garrison. My mind and body were in between ecstasy and reality. I felt Bryson increase his thrusts. Then he put my other leg on his shoulders, and I felt him go deeper inside me. Now he was slamming into me with more force. I looked at him, and his eyes were closed, and his face looked tense.

"Bryson, baby slow down."

He ignored me, and the hard slamming continued. It didn't feel amazing anymore and was becoming painful. I tried lowering my legs, but his strength prevented my legs from moving. Then he grunted. He let my legs down, more like slammed them down and turned me on my side and slid back inside of me. His stroke was violent. I felt him pull my hair hard and my neck jerked. My moans were no longer of ecstasy but from discomfort. Bryson didn't care and didn't stop. Then it clicked. Aunt Gladys' evil spirit was amongst us, and he was reliving the birthday gift she'd given him each year. I wondered how long she molested him. Did he seek counseling? Is this what I had to look forward to if there was a future for us? I heard him grunt again and he let my hair go. His hands were gripping my hips tightly. So tight I felt he was going to break the skin. I tried my plea once more.

"Bryson, baby it's okay. She's not here anymore."

"No!" he yelled.

"Baby you have to stop now, you're hurting me," I said.

"I love you, Sam."

In the midst of his battle with Aunt Gladys, somehow I believed his words. I mentally checked out and let him commemorate his cruel birthday memories.

"I love you, Sam. Damn it."

He was battling demons I couldn't comprehend. He yelled out as I felt him climaxing inside of me. I heard him breathing heavily as he lay on the side of me holding me tight. I was afraid and happy.

When I felt his embrace soften, I got up and went to my bathroom to shower. I had been in the shower a few minutes before Bryson joined me. My fear returned. I was ready for him to return to Germany but when he stepped into the shower, he did something I wasn't expecting.

"Sam, I'm truly sorry. I don't know what happened."

Then he kissed me, hugged me, and started crying on my shoulder. I didn't know the last time Bryson cried but the way he stood in my shower crying, it felt like it had been an eternity. The water splashed on our bodies, and Bryson sat down. I stood there for a few seconds remembering being in the same position from someone's hurt towards me. I didn't yell at Alexa this time instead I joined Bryson and sat between his legs. He wrapped his arms around me and again said, "Sam I'm so sorry. I want things to be perfect with us. I hope I haven't ruined it."

I couldn't respond at that moment because I wasn't sure there was going to be an *us*. Instead, I rested my hand on his arm and closed my eyes.

When I opened my eyes, I was in bed naked and alone. I looked at the digital clock, and it read 2:22 AM. I sat up and turned on my night lamp. I didn't see Bryson's luggage on the side of the room where it had been. I got out of bed and walked to the guest bedroom. He wasn't there either. I came back to the kitchen and turned on the light. On the counter was the answer to my question. I walked over and picked up the piece of white bond paper.

My dearest Samantha,

I'm truly sorry for allowing my demons to enter your place of peace and any physical discomfort when we had intercourse. I'm ashamed and embarrassed. I have gone to check into a hotel by the airport and will return to Germany in the morning. I hope you can forgive me and will one day want to see me again. I love you, Samantha Hunt, like I've never loved anyone before.
Bryson.

His words resonated in me as I read his note repeatedly. I don't know why I was standing there crying, but I couldn't stop. Each time I read his note, I dissected another piece of it and evaluated its meaning. His note said he loved me, yet he didn't say what hotel he was checking into or which flight he was catching. I took that to mean he didn't want me to contact him before he left. At least William told me he was moving to New York. I stood in my kitchen a few minutes more before throwing Bryson's escape letter in the trash. I went back to my bedroom and laid in bed a few minutes before falling back asleep.

Chapter 28

My alarm sounded a few hours later waking me from restless hours of sleep. I checked my cell phone, and there were no missed calls, emails or text messages from Bryson. I got dressed and went downstairs to the gym. I tried working out to get my mind going in a positive direction instead of letting the devil's workshop put in overtime hours. It was no use because my mind kept replaying his note in my head. I began to wonder if he was really returning to Germany or was visiting me a pit stop en route to see his ex-girlfriend; was she really his ex? I increased the speed to 7.0 on the treadmill. I started comparing things he said to things William said. The speed of my thoughts was breaking world records. I thought about Trent for some reason and the possibilities I may have missed. He was such a nice guy. I slowed the speed of the treadmill and started my cool down.

When I got back upstairs, I made myself a cup of hot tea before I showered. I sat on one of the stools in my kitchen watching the sun wake up. I decided I wasn't going to the office and was going to enjoy my time off and catch up with Carrie. I stepped into my shower, and as the hot water began to touch my body, I said aloud *'This shower is becoming a place of misery.'* Inside the shower, I came to the conclusion I needed to make one phone call before I planned anything with Carrie. When I stepped out of the shower, I heard my phone ringing. I stopped drying off and rushed to the side of my bed. The call was from a random number. I stood there as water dripped onto the carpet and frowned. I sat down on the side of my bed looking at the phone tempted to answer it. I didn't recognize the number, but I knew who it was. William's timing couldn't have been better. No, don't answer it Sam. I crossed my legs and bit my bottom lip. The phone stopped ringing, and I exhaled and gave myself a pat on the back for the little bit of courage I mustered up. I was completely dry, but I returned to my bathroom to floss and brush my teeth. When I got back to my room, I picked up my cell phone and scrolled to the B's. I hadn't spoken to my therapist, Dr. Brooks in over a year. I started seeing her after William and I broke up. I dialed the upper Northwest DC office number and left a message for her to call me.

"Good morning!"

"Hi, Sam! How's it going?"

"He's leaving today. You want to hang out?"

"What happened?" Carrie asked.

"I'll tell you all about it over lunch," I said.

"Okay. Are we driving one car or meeting somewhere?" Carrie asked.

"I can pick you up," I told her.

"Sounds good see you around noon?" Carrie asked.

"Perfect."

"I'm sorry things didn't work out Sam."

"It's okay. See you soon."

"Okay."

When I hung up with my best friend, I wasn't sure calling her immediately had been a good idea. I didn't want to tell her all that happened, but I knew Carrie would want details. I looked at the time on my cell phone and hoped Dr. Brooks would call me as soon as she got my message and that she had an appointment available this morning.

I got on the Internet and paid some bills and watched some recorded television shows. I scrolled to Trent's name in my phone and started a text message but quickly deleted it before sending. Where are you Dr. Brooks? I was in the middle of watching an episode of Scandal when my cell phone rang. I looked at the caller id, and it was a call I surely wanted but wasn't sure I wanted to answer now. My cell phone rang a few more times.

"Hello!" I said.

Silence on the other but I could hear background noise of gate changes, flight arrivals and a Mr. Don to pick up the nearest paging phone.

"Are you okay Bryson?" I asked.

"Yes but I...."

He didn't complete his sentence. I held the phone and didn't try to help him. The silence was so uncomfortable.

"Sam I'm sorry," he said.

The way he said it felt much different from what I read. I was still annoyed though.

"Yes, I read that in your note."

I heard the announcement for his flight to board in the background. The destination was Frankfurt. My thoughts of a pit stop were canceled.

"Sam I'll go to counseling. I just...."

Again he couldn't finish his sentence.

"Bryson what would you go to counseling for?"

Silence.

"Because, because... I don't want to lose you," he said.

"Bryson we are just getting to know each other. If you go to counseling, it needs to be for your own betterment."

He didn't say anything.

"So are you leaving me?" he asked.

"You decided to leave. I didn't ask you to."

"I know. I was just nervous and afraid."

"Nervous and afraid of what? I told you it was okay," I said.

"My behavior was unacceptable."

"Which part?" I asked.

"All of it."

"You can't control the dreams, but you had a choice when I asked you to stop when we were having sex."

More silence but I heard *'now boarding group 2'*.

"Sam, can we fix this?"

My phone beeped. It was Dr. Brooks calling.

"Bryson, board your flight I need to take this call. If you don't mind doing so, text me to let me know you made it home. Have a safe flight."

I didn't want to be rude but I needed to take this call, and we weren't going to solve anything prior to the doors closing for his flight. I switched over to Dr. Brooks.

"Hello."

"Good morning Ms. Hunt. I got your message. What can I do for you?" Dr. Brooks asked.

I skipped all of the telephone etiquettes.

"Do you have any appointments available this morning?"

"Let me check. I do have a 9 AM today. Would you like to come in at that time?" she asked.

I had said yes right after I heard the time.

"Is your insurance still the same Ms. Hunt?"

"Yes, it is."

"I'll see you at 9 this morning."

"Thank you."

"You're welcome," she said.

After the call disconnected, I called Bryson back, but the call went to his voicemail. I didn't leave a message.

I was able to find a parking spot a couple of blocks over from Dr. Brooks' office. I wasn't in the same state of mind I was when I first started seeing her, but I had an eerie feeling walking up the street to her row house office. I saw people walking their dogs, some just leisurely walking and others jogging. I wondered if they knew the row house Dr. Brooks occupied was for unstable, emotional people like me. I rang the doorbell, and she appeared smiling and wearing the same large framed glasses I remembered.

"Good morning Ms. Hunt. Come in."

"Good morning," I said.

Her office was painted light grey with frameless pictures of exotic flowers. She had a black leather sofa with two matching sunken chairs. In the corner by the shaded window was a large plant. Once patients chose their place of confession, she'd sit. Her desk didn't have any personal effects just a laptop, a few books, pens and writing tablets. She sat across from me with a pen and one of her writing tablets.

"So Ms. Hunt it's been awhile. How are things?"

She knew how things were if I was in her office. I didn't answer right away. She didn't ask the question again. Her face was young looking, and she maintained her smile while I pondered my obvious answer.

"Things are good."

I saw her write something on her tablet. I picked at one of my nails, a nervous condition since I was a child.

"The last time we spoke you had moved on from your fiancé and had started dating."

"Yes."

One word answers are always dead giveaways.

"Are you still dating?"

"Yes."

She wrote something else on her tablet and put the pen down. She crossed her legs and said, "Ms. Hunt, what would you like to talk about this morning?"

I looked away before answering. My finger would have bled if I kept picking it.

"I'm dating someone."

"That's good. How's it going?"

"It's long distance, and I think I see red flags."

Dr. Brooks picked up her pen and wrote on the tablet.

"Why do you say that?" she asked.

"He came to visit me and left abruptly."

"Where does he live?" she asked.

"Germany," I said.

"Oh, that's quite a distance," she said as she wrote.

"Yes, it is," I confirmed.

"How long have you guys been dating?" she asked.

"Six or seven months."

"Relatively still new. How many times have you seen each other?"

"Three if you include the introduction."

"I see. What happened while he was visiting you that caused him to leave abruptly?" Was it work or did you guys get into an argument?" she asked.

"It wasn't work," I said.

"What was the argument over?" she asked.

"It wasn't an argument either," I said.

She wrote on that damn tablet.

"Why don't you tell me what happened Ms. Hunt?"

"He came to visit for his birthday."

"And?"

"You want to know everything?"

"Enough to know what lead up to him leaving abruptly."

"To be honest, I really don't know why he left."

"Have you two had intercourse?"

"Yes, we have."

"And how's that?"

"What do you mean exactly?"

Is it pleasing to both of you?"

"Yes, it is."

"But what Ms. Hunt?"

She still knew me and could read my thoughts. I paused before continuing.

"Ms. Hunt?"

"Bryson says he was molested by a family member for years."

"So, his name is Bryson?"

"Yes, and while he was sleeping, he started having nightmares."

"Yes," she said as she wrote. "And then what happened?" she asked.

"We stayed in, ordered food, and watched Netflix."

"How long had he been here before this happened?"

This was starting to feel like a police interrogation. I forgot you have to give some insight before your treatment plan could begin and fifty minutes flies by.

"A few days," I said.

"Had you two had intercourse? Was the performance lacking or were the two of you uncomfortable with the situation?"

"It was great but after the nightmare not so great. The intercourse started off passionate then turned violent," I said.

"Did you tell Bryson to stop?" she asked looking over the top of her glasses.

"I did."

"Did he?"

"No."

She put her pen down and gave me a concerning look. I saw her look at the desk clock. I looked as well, and it was 9:40. She uncrossed her legs and rested her hands on top of the writing tablet. "Ms. Hunt, are you going to see Bryson again?"

"I'm not sure," I said.

"Do you want to?" she asked.

I didn't answer.

"Ms. Hunt, do you feel like Bryson raped you?" she asked.

"No, I don't feel that way," I said.

"What do you feel?" she asked.

"I really like him, but I'm concerned about how he deals with that particular issue."

"So you think the nightmare and him being molested played a part in the rough sex?"

"Yes."

She looked at me in silence a few seconds, but it felt like an eternity before she spoke. "Unfortunately that's our time. Would you like to schedule another appointment in a week?"

She grabbed her brown leather calendar book and started giving me dates and times available. After William, I didn't think I'd ever see Dr. Brooks again.

"Yes please put me down for 9 AM every week."

"Okay, Ms. Hunt I put you down for 9 AM and six sessions to start."

Dr. Brooks stood with a big smile, extended her hand and wished me a great day. I shook her hand and thanked her.

Chapter 29

I felt some relief after leaving Dr. Brooks' office. I had to put on a different face for Carrie. I didn't want her worrying about me and jeopardizing her pregnancy. I was looking forward to being a godmother to her son. She had decided on the name Connor Aiden but was still unclear on whether she was going to give him Jonathan's last name or hers. I called and told her I was downstairs.

"Hey, Sam!"

"Hi there, mama to be."

"Girl I'm starving. Where are we going?" she asked.

"How about Legal Seafood in Tysons?"

"Sounds good. So what happened Sam?" she asked.

I pulled into traffic before repeating what I'd just told my shrink. "How's the pregnancy going?" I asked.

"So far so good. I can't hold my bladder like I used too." She laughed.

"Have you heard from Jonathan?" I asked.

"Have you?" she asked.

"You know I haven't," I said.

"That's your answer," she said.

"He'll come around Carrie."

"I'm over it, Sam. What happened with Bryson?"

"Well… he has an issue that he doesn't know how to deal with."

"What the heck does that mean?"

"Carrie if you ever meet him you can't repeat any of this."

I used the word "if" leaving the door of possibility open. Carrie put up some sort of finger sign to show honor. I laughed. "Girl you weren't a girl scout," I said.

"Yeah well, I promise not to say anything."

"One of the nights he was here I woke up to him tossing and turning."

"So he had a bad dream," she said.

"Well, he says one of his aunts molested him and this happens occasionally."

"Okay. Did he hit you or something?"

I laughed. "You know better than that."

We pulled up to Legal Seafood and valet parked. Carrie got out of the car and told me, "I have to pee when we get inside, but you need to get to the reason why things didn't work out. Right now you're not making any sense."

I grabbed the parking ticket from the valet and headed to the restaurant behind Carrie. I got us a booth facing the inside of the mall. I ordered two waters and told the waiter my friend should be back soon.

"Okay, girl I feel so much better. I just peed before you picked me up. So what happened?" she asked as she caught her breath.

"We were having sex, and it got rough. I asked him to stop, and he didn't," I said.

Carrie had a blank stare on her face.

"So you didn't like it Sam?"

I didn't know how to answer because at the time I felt like I was torn between pleasure and being a psychiatrist. "I thought he was having memories of the family member who molested him and taking it out on me."

"Are you serious?" Carrie said.

"Yes because it was after the nightmare."

"Sam, no offense but I don't think one had to do with the other."

"No? Why do you say that?"

"Sam sometimes men don't want to be so delicate in the bedroom. You said he was super nice in Dallas and on the phone right?"

"Yes I did that's why it caught me off guard, and I didn't know how to respond."

"I think you're overreacting."

"Okay, how do you explain him leaving in the middle of the night?" I asked.

"That's a good question. Maybe he didn't know how to talk to you about it," Carrie said.

"Perhaps you're right," I said.

When the waiter returned, Carrie ordered a 16 oz. steak with a baked potato and Caesar salad. I ordered the grilled shrimp with asparagus.

"I thought something happened with his ex-girlfriend," Carrie said as she ate one of the rolls with butter.

"No, I don't believe he heard from her anymore," I said.

"So, are you done with him?" Carrie asked.

"I don't know, to be honest," I said.

"Why not? One misunderstanding and you dismiss him?" Carrie asked.

"What if it's more than one issue?" I asked.

"Sam you're looking for the impossible."

"Oh yeah, what's the impossible?" I asked.

"The perfect person!" she said eating her salad. "Does he treat you good?" she asked. "Does he make you feel like nothing or no one else matters?" she continued. "All I've been hearing is how great Bryson is. Now after a bad night of sleep and a little rough sex you're done? Sam, I think you're wrong on this one," Carrie said.

I felt like I was in an extended therapy session but without a co-pay. "I'll see how things go from here."

We finished eating lunch and walked through the mall looking at baby clothes and enjoying each other's company. After we left the mall, we stopped by Sweet Frogs for some frozen yogurt. While we were eating our yogurt, Carrie's cell phone rang. She showed me the caller id. It was Jonathan. She didn't answer and didn't listen to the message he left.

"When are you going to talk to him?" I asked.

"We can talk after the birth of my son. I'm not trying to be stressed, and I'm not having sex with him," she said.

"Okay but what if he wants to go to your appointments and Lamaze class with you?"

"I thought you were going with me, Sam?" she asked.

"I am but if the father of your child offers don't you think you should at least entertain it?" I asked.

She pulled out her cell phone and played his voicemail on speaker, so I could hear it.

Hi, Carrie, I hope you're doing well. Can we talk soon? This is Jonathan.

"See he didn't ask about my appointments or the baby. Can we talk is code for can we have sex?" she said.

I shook my head and laughed at my best friend. "You should return his phone call and take some of the advice you gave me as you devour that steak," I said.

"Touché!"

I dropped Carrie off and headed to the bookstore to pick up a good book to read. I hadn't been to the bookstore in a while, and I immediately felt good looking at all the intriguing books by millions of talented authors. I browsed the new releases in fiction then the must read table. I picked up a book titled Neighborhood Watch and read the back cover. The story seemed interesting, so I stood there and read a few chapters. I headed towards the checkout with the must read fiction novel in my hand.

When I got home, I poured a glass of Shiraz and retired to my sofa and continued reading Neighborhood Watch. I got halfway through before I started feeling tired. I took a shower and got in bed. My ringing cell phone woke me from my sleep. I picked up my cell phone and saw it was Bryson calling. I had asked him to text me when he landed but I wasn't ready to talk to him. I let my cell phone continue to ring until my automated voicemail picked up. I didn't listen to the message. I turned over and went back to sleep.

Chapter 30

Today was one of the prettiest days I could remember in a long time, however, a dark cloud hovered over me this afternoon.

"Thank you for having lunch with me," he said.

"You're welcome."

I returned William's call and agreed to meet him for lunch. I felt that would be safe and I had a 50/50 chance of not ending up in his condo at the newly renovated wharf.

"So how have you been since I last saw you with your boyfriend?"

"Fine."

He smiled. He too knew what my one-word answers meant.

"Seriously Sam, are you happy with him?"

The waiter appeared to take our drink order and answered my SOS. William ordered me a vodka and tonic. He ordered bourbon on the rocks. We knew each other so well, yet the deep-rooted pain still felt fresh as I sat there. I looked away because it was hard to make eye contact with him. He sat across from me happy as a kid visiting the happiest place on earth for the first time. I didn't return Bryson's calls, nor did I reply to his text messages and emails.

"Did you take on the deal in Charles County?" I asked.

"It's in the works," William said.

He reached across the table to touch my hand. I pulled my hand back. "William, don't please."

"Okay, Sam."

I don't know if it was the way he said 'okay Sam' or me finally realizing this was pointless but when the waiter returned with our drinks, I took a sip of my drink then stood up and said, "William I apologize for wasting your time."

"Sam I'm sorry."

"Stop saying that. You sound like a broken record. Can you say something else?" I was annoyed at myself for even being here. He sat there with a blank look on his face. "Don't worry about paying for my drink. I'll take care of the bill on my way out."

"Sam, please don't leave," he said.

He was looking pathetic to me now, and I lost all respect for him at that very moment. I didn't say anything else to him. I walked to the bar, paid the bill, and left.

As I waited for the valet to bring my car, I called Bryson. The phone didn't ring a full ring before I heard his voice.

"Sam, are you okay?"

I saw William exiting the restaurant and walking towards me. I saw the look of shame on his face. When he saw me on the phone, something told me he knew I was talking to Bryson. "Yes. I'm fine. Sorry I missed your calls."

"Did you get my texts and emails?"

"Yes, I did. Bryson, I needed some time to clear my head."

He didn't say anything. William was now standing close enough to hear my conversation. He didn't say anything to me though. He gave the valet his ticket and stood there silently looking at me. The valet pulled up with my car. I saw William approach the driver's side of my car. I quickly told Bryson I'd call him back. When William got close, I felt myself getting weak all over again. He thanked the valet and held my door open for me. Our eyes were locked on each other as I slowly walked to get in my car.

"Goodbye, Sam," he said.

He extended his hand for me to shake. I couldn't take my eyes off of him. I put my purse inside my car and hugged him tightly. I felt him slowly bring his hands up to hug me. At that moment everything we'd ever done flashed before my eyes - the good and bad times, the engagement, the abortion, the countless tears I'd cried, and the times I fell victim to his empty promises and the shameful times we had sex when I knew that was all it was. I started to cry, and William tried to pull back to look at me. I kept my tight embrace so he couldn't see my face. After I stopped crying, I loosened my grip around him and stepped back.

"Sam," he said.

I covered his lips. I didn't want to hear another apology. Enough had been said. I took one last look at him. "Goodbye, William Henry Randolph. I will probably always love you, but it's time for my mind, body, and soul to heal."

He lowered his head. I got into my car and didn't look at him. He closed my door, and I slowly drove away. I saw him in my rearview mirror still standing by the valet looking in my direction. I called Bryson back. His voice was still calm.

"What's going on Sam?"

"It's late over there. Let's talk tomorrow," I suggested.

"I'm not sleepy. Talk to me please," he said.

Time to heal Sam.

"Bryson, I met William for lunch today."

"Oh, I see. Are you guys getting back together?" he asked. His voice was stern.

"No."

"Then why did you meet him?"

"He called right after you left abruptly and I thought I needed to see him."

"So because I left, you ran to him?"

Men can be so dramatic at times.

"Bryson, my head was in a tailspin."

"So now what, Sam?"

"I'm not going back to William."

"But are you with me?"

"I want to be but."

"But what?"

"I'm scared."

"I told you I would get counseling Sam."

"Are you doing that for yourself or me?" I asked.

He didn't say anything. "Sam I know I need to address my issues. I've been in denial for too long."

"Bryson I'm not judging you. I just want you to get help if and only if you feel you need it," I said.

"I need it Sam. I love you."

I wasn't ready to say those three words.

"How do you know you love me?"

"Because I know what I feel when I talk to you, when I don't talk to you, and how much I miss you."

"Are you sure it's not just infatuation?"

"Sam, I know what love is. I'm sorry you've been hurt so bad that you've given up on love."

"Bryson I'm open to taking things slow if you're okay with that."

"I'm not going anywhere Sam. I want to be with you for the rest of my life."

I bit my bottom lip and saw his handsome face and thought about the way he kissed me in Dallas for the first time. "Bryson, thank you for being patient."

"I'll never give up on you or us, Sam."

"Are you sure about that?"

"Yes, I am."

"Bryson you should get some sleep, and we can talk tomorrow."

"You promise? No more disappearing acts?"

"Yes, I promise. I missed hearing your voice," I said.

"Sam."

"Yes?"

"Will you come see me for Christmas?"

"We can see how things go, Bryson."

"Okay, Sam."

We disconnected, and I drove the rest of the way home in silence.

Bryson and I continued talking every day as we had been. He told me that he started seeing a therapist over in Germany. I never told him about my weekly appointments with Dr. Brooks. He continued to ask me to visit for the Christmas holiday, but I didn't commit to visiting. I liked where we were in our relationship. Carrie gave birth to Connor Aiden Richards (Jonathan's last name). I didn't hear from William again, but I saw him one afternoon in Georgetown with a young lady. He saw me but didn't smile or acknowledge our acquaintance. I was happy to see him with someone. My weekly appointments with Dr. Brooks were helping me greatly. I was slowly healing and felt like I was ready to give love another chance with Bryson. He told me he loved me every time we hung up and never once got upset when I didn't tell him the same. I often think about Ms. Boote and what she said about love while we were 35,000 feet in the air and smile. "Love can put all the pieces back together, stronger than before…."

About the author

Bestselling Author James H. Waggoner is a Southern California native, born in Los Angeles. He attended the University of Maryland where he earned a degree in Management Studies. James served in the U.S. Air Force for 20 years and has lived in 12 different countries. James writes his nail biting stories to capture avid readers from the first page and keep them on the edge of their seats until the end. His vivid imagination brings the characters on the page to real life. His stories are sure to give you passion, love, hate, heart beating action and a deep message to ponder long after you've finished reading his latest masterpiece.

James is active in his community with youth sports as a youth sports basketball coach and mentor. James has been a featured author and panelist at the National Book Club Conference sharing his experiences as a self- published author. He is a proud member of Omega Psi Phi Fraternity, Inc. When he's not writing, you will find James spending time with his family and friends, traveling, golfing or enjoying a fine cigar. He resides in Northern Virginia.

Contact

Email: authorjameshwaggoner@gmail.com
Web: www.jameshwaggoner.net
Facebook:
https://www.facebook.com/EmptySoulForHire/?fref=ts
Amazon: http://amzn.to/2kGYYLa

Thank you for reading my book. I would be most grateful if you would leave a review.
Amazon: http://amzn.to/2kGYYLa

James.

Made in the USA
Middletown, DE
26 April 2018